Loom

ARAB AMERICAN WRITING

Other titles in Arab American Writing

Loom

A Novel

THÉRÈSE
SOUKAR
CHEHADE

Syracuse University Press

First Edition 2010
10 11 12 13 14 15   6 5 4 3 2 1

∞ The paper used in this publication meets the minimum requirements of the American
National Standard for Information Sciences—Permanence of Paper for Printed Library
Materials, ANSI Z39.48-1992.

For a listing of books published and distributed by Syracuse University Press,
visit our Web site at SyracuseUniversityPress.syr.edu.

ISBN: 978-0-8156-0982-7

Library of Congress Cataloging-in-Publication Data
Chehade, Thérèse Soukar.
    Loom / Thérèse Soukar Chehade. — 1st ed.
       p. cm. — (Arab American writing)
    ISBN 978-0-8156-0982-7 (pbk. : alk. paper)
    1. Lebanese Americans—Fiction.   2. Lebanese American women—Fiction.
3. Mothers and daughters—Fiction.   4. Immigrants—United States—Fiction.
5. Neighbors—Fiction.   I. Title.
    PS3603.H44557L66 2010
    813'.6—dc22   2010037304

Manufactured in the United States of America

For James and Nicholas, two wonderful boys

◆   ◆   ◆

THÉRÈSE SOUKAR CHEHADE was born and raised in Beirut, Lebanon. She received her M.F.A. from the University of Massachusetts, Amherst. She lives in Massachusetts with her family. *Loom* is her first novel.

Acknowledgments

My deepest thanks go to my UMass "babes" group and longtime friends: Justine Dymond, Tamara Grogan, Nicole Nemec, Elizabeth Porto, Kamila Shamsie, and Pamela Thompson. It has been my great fortune to know you.

Thank you to Mara Bright, Valerie Brinkmann, Pam Richardson, and Cynthia Waring of the Bear Mountain Writers group for listening to excerpts from this novel and finding the good parts; to Tayeb El-Hibri, who read and responded to my e-mails and provided a sea of resources; to everyone at Syracuse University Press who helped with the publication of this novel, particularly to Mary Selden Evans for her faith and enthusiasm; to all the writers and teachers whose words still echo in my imagination.

To my family, you have my deep gratitude for your unflagging support. To Nadim, thank you for patiently answering my questions. And to my mother: you paved the way.

Arabic Terms

habibti: my love (feminine)

inshallah: God willing

kaa'k: Bread in the shape of a pouch with a small handle. *Zaatar* may be sprinkled through a hole the vendor makes in the bread.

kafta: ground meat seasoned with parsley and onions.

kazoz: soda.

khalti: my maternal aunt.

labneh: strained yogurt.

man'oosheh: flat bread seasoned with *zaatar. Mana'eesh* is the plural form.

sitt: madam

teta: grandma

zaatar: dried thyme mixed with spices and herbs. Olive oil is added to form a paste.

Loom

EVA IS COMING. Her laughter rings in Emilie's memory. She remembers the girl's thick hair falling to her shoulders (although no longer a girl; Eva has been a woman for a long time now), a red headband keeping it away from her face. Her plaid blue and gray school uniform is mostly what she remembers her in, and those droopy navy blue knee socks slipping down her legs like gravity was dragging them, when in fact it was Eva herself who had pulled and stretched to make the elastic give, to make those socks fall and show more skin.

On the night table, the clock ticks. This time, the waiting is for a purpose. Soon, a line will be drawn between here and there, past and present. The past will be made flesh, and Eva will emerge and ask with her usual liveliness, Khalti Emilie, have you straightened out those Americans yet?

The morning breaks slowly, casting its gray light on the fields swollen with snow. Emilie makes her way to the window, pulling her black woolen shawl about her more from habit than actual chill. Her view is obstructed by the white blur the wind has whipped up. From memory, she makes out where the farm stands behind the cornfields and where the road loops around the hill then drops into a sharp descent all the way to Main Street. Only the tall trees and the church's steeple are saved from the general drowning.

Will Eva notice how different the sky is here, as if the breaths of the people living under it rise together to paint it a different blue, a different gray? When Emilie saw it the first time, she couldn't tell exactly where the difference lay. Seemed like she was already losing her memory, slowly becoming submerged in the new skittering light. Seemed like the land stretching ahead was too big not to disappear into, and she a speck tumbling down the sloping earth.

At 7:05, she looks at a point on the horizon where she thinks her niece's plane must be landing at that precise minute. Is she expecting her to emerge from the whiteness and, taking huge leaps toward the house, to stand before her as the incarnation of the past, untouched by separation?

She dozes, waking every once in a while to look at the brooding sky. It is nearly eight when the ring jolts her awake. She knows it is Eva even before she picks up the phone in the hallway.

"I'm in New York and will be coming as soon as I can," Eva says. "All planes are cancelled on account of the storm. I miss you so, Khalti!"

When they talked on the phone before, a scratch in the line, the background noise when Eva called, usually from a public Centrale, reminded them that their communication, Eva in Beirut and Emilie in Vermont, was miraculous and fragile. Emilie would press her ear into the phone, as if doing so made her closer to her niece. She would remember the white walls in the Centrale, the small ceiling fans stirring up an ineffectual breeze, and the people listless with the heat, shuffling through to the next available phone. This morning, Eva's voice rings clear. Stark, somehow, without the usual undercurrent of noise.

Yet she is near. But for the blizzard she would be here. And at this, touched by joy, Emilie gives herself to it, laughs and chatters, samples at the feast of words before her.

And then it is gone. Slips off her like a beautiful gown, and at once Emilie's shoulders sink. What, a moment ago, was Eva's nearness is again huge distance. Emilie lifts her head and sees her daughter leaning against the wall waiting her turn to talk, and hands her the receiver.

Back in her room, Emilie tidies up to pass the time. She smoothes a ripple in the bedspread, a blue mercerized cotton coverlet with a diamond pattern in the middle she had brought with her from Lebanon, pushes a chair against the window and sits. Folding her hands in her lap, she waits for the house to wake.

A world hopeful under its thick blanket of snow. A world cleaned to the bone, at the ready. More waiting. At her age, this is no less than hateful.

JOSEPHINE PRESSES HER SHOULDER against the wall, tapping an unlit cigarette against the heel of her hand. Her mother's words reach her through the haze of the sleepless night she has spent, finally dozing off for what seemed like seconds before being wakened by the ring. Josephine feels the last wisps of sleep dissolve, replaced by a new resolve, something like expectation, for there is her mother now chattering in a way she hasn't since they left Beirut, and Josephine is comforted by the loose strands of hair escaping her mother's eternal bun and grazing her cheeks, and by the way this gives her a youthful, pleasingly rumpled look. All will be well.

When it is her turn to talk, Josephine half expects to hear a tearful Eva on the other end, lost in great big New York. "Picking December to fly halfway across the globe isn't exactly a good idea," she'd said when Eva called a week earlier to announce she had booked a flight to Boston via Rome and New York. "New England's weather can't be relied on," she'd quickly added, afraid she might have sounded inhospitable. Last night, when the snow had started to thud the windows and the weatherman had predicted nearly three feet of accumulation, Josephine thought how she might just remind Eva of their conversation.

Eva frets a little about being delayed, but otherwise she sounds cheerful. Still the resilient one. Josephine is proud and irritated that this must always be so. She would have liked to be the one to comfort, to pull away from the brink.

"All this snow! I couldn't bear it."

Josephine feels a flash of annoyance as if she herself was found difficult to bear, but her voice is cheerful when she responds. "Don't worry, dear, these storms are short-lived." And, after a pause: "We can't wait to see you."

When the conversation shifts to practical matters, Josephine is all business, knotting her brows in concentration and fishing out pen and paper from the drawer to jot down the number of the hotel where Eva is staying, and going once again over her bus itinerary from Boston to Scarabee with a precision gained from many rehearsals. When the time comes, she is counting on impressing her cousin with her knowledge, the ease with which names of American towns and cities roll off her tongue. She enunciates the names of these stops with the finest American accent she can muster after eighteen years, whispering through the remainder of their conversation, careful not to wake her brother and his wife who are sleeping on the first floor. As for Marie, her young niece, she can sleep through an earthquake.

Back in her room, she lights up a cigarette and rotates her head to work the stiffness out of her neck. The small bones in her neck crack in a succession of minute explosions.

She goes over the things she might tell her cousin. "How thrilling it was, my dear," she would begin, "to be able to leave the house at any hour without fearing the bombs."

Yet how dull it soon became. The days repetitive, distinguished only by their names on the calendar, the meals that Salma cooks, the seasons, their growing garden, and now the lines on her skin. George franchised a convenience store soon after they settled in Scarabee. It has been both their saving grace and a noose around her neck. She's forty-four. Time's been stealing the days.

She walks over to the window and opens the curtains. She is not surprised to see Loom outside, digging a path in his front yard, a big pile of fresh snow to his side. His house is set back from the road some two hundred feet and just about the same distance from the brush that divides their properties. Today, screened by snow, he looks like a murky figure in a grainy old black-and-white movie, a ghostly image surrounded by a haze of white.

She could tell Eva about him, how she watches him every chance she gets, how he's in her dreams. Yet she'd be hard pressed to describe him or tell her his name.

It was Marie who first called him Loom. Sometimes, Marie and Josephine watch him in his backyard, pruning, picking at ice, or working on his old car. She imagines walking casually to him and inviting him for coffee and pastries.

Marie says he has a big shadow for someone so short. "There is more to old Loom than meets the eye," she concludes. Even though Marie calls him old, Josephine is not at all sure about his age. The two women steal glances at him when they mow the lawn and trim the lilac bushes next to the brush that divides their properties. Sometimes he quickly tips his hat in their direction, but mostly he doesn't acknowledge them, carrying on with the various upkeep jobs that seem to require most of his time.

He wears a hat all year, a woolen one in cold weather, the kind the seamen wear in the French movies. Marie says there is something strange about a man who will not let you see the top of his head. Josephine tells her he is probably bald. But Marie prefers her own version.

Josephine has no time to dwell on this last thought. Marie walks in looking for cigarettes and flops down on the bed without removing her slippers. Josephine pulls off the offending items and lays them on the floor by the bed.

Marie chatters on. Eva's phone call has wakened her after all. "There is old Loom again," she says, pointing at the window. There's not much going on in this house to rouse the girl's imagination, so she takes her thrills where she finds them. A bit like me, Josephine thinks. Needing to rise above the tedium of daily life. But Josephine flies real low, just enough to make both the rising and landing invisible to others.

Marie inhales deeply and Josephine feels guilty for allowing this corruption of her niece's young lungs. At eighteen, she is a child. A beauty. She has the auburn curls and small face of someone from a past century.

Screwing their faces through the smoke, the two women watch Loom shovel, even though the forecast predicted the storm would last through the night. Strong wind drifts the new snow down to the fields.

What keeps him outdoors?

"Suppose he is hiding a corpse inside?" Marie asks.

"Who knows," Josephine replies.

"You can always count on old Loom," Marie says, blowing smoke through her nose.

Loom had bought the house a year earlier. The previous owners were pleasant but territorial. Thick brush separated their plots and gave the illusion of natural boundaries. But their land expanded beyond the brush, well into the vegetable patch that Josephine and her mother, foregoing property lines, planted every May for years. One day the neighbors cleared the brush and slowly circled the patch. Josephine dug out the tomatoes and the cabbage, but the neighbors did not plant new dividers. After they left, the house was several months for sale before Loom bought it. He cut the brush, which had in the meantime proliferated undisturbed. Later, it grew back. When their new neighbor did not show signs of trimming it, Josephine became curious, then watchful, and finally convinced that he would prove to be as transient as the tourists who flocked to their town every summer. The rest of his property was meticulously trimmed, and the profusion at the edges seemed to be a sign of deep contradictions.

Marie named him Loom one day in October, when the maple was ablaze with color. The two women were having breakfast on the deck, the weak morning sun making a pretense of warming them through their shawls and thin cotton dresses. Loom was replacing old shingles on his roof. That summer he had painted the house buttery yellow and the shutters dark green. Marie said he had been showing up in her dreams. "Now I will run away for sure," she said. She had been talking about leaving Scarabee, but that morning she seemed more determined than usual. Dreaming about strangers, inventing sinister names. Perhaps she was right. The time had come to move on.

Marie added that Loom also meant something else, but she did not say precisely what it was. Later, Josephine looked up the word in secret. She is ashamed of her English, still barely adequate after all these years. She remembered the only time she had seen a loom during the summer of her sixteenth birthday. Her mother's house in the mountains where they spent their summer vacation was undergoing repairs, and they had rented a house in a small village on the coast near Beirut. Their landlady wove sweaters for her children on an old loom. The sweaters were beige and brown, colors that must have been on sale at the local store. A few finished ones sat stiffly in a heap on a chair. Josephine had trouble imagining that beautiful coastal village turning so cold in the winter, it required such ugly sweaters.

It was during that summer that she and George declared war on each other. He was thirteen and covetous. She was relentlessly stamping out competition, taking great care to show him who was boss. Over the years they would make peace sporadically, short periods during which they were quiet and wary, then snap out again into ruthless combat. In America they quieted down, in a particular, businesslike way, two people surviving side by side, relying on each other to see the next day through.

Eva spent that summer with them. She was often ill and rarely left the room she shared with Josephine. Josephine was surprised (Eva was usually fit as a horse), but not in the least bit saddened. That year she had finally convinced her mother to buy her a bikini to replace the old one-piece suit she had been wearing since she was thirteen. She walked proudly to the beach every morning in her yellow and green suit, conscious that she was turning heads, until Eva, feeling better one day, came out looking stunning in a simple black bikini, her body all beguiling dips and curves. Josephine felt the crushing pangs of jealousy. She ran to her room and flung herself down on her bed, the new suit torn off and hurled furiously across the room.

Although she had every intention of spending the rest of her life in hiding, she came out a few hours later, already bored and looking for something to do. The rest of their vacation proved uneventful, and Josephine forgot her disappointment and was once again swept by the summer. They left the village in the middle of September, with the sky a perfect blue. In the car, Eva slept and George put algae in Josephine's sandwich and rocks on her lap, but she ignored him, her head filled with their vacation and the smells of bleach and strawberry preserves and wet sand caught in the grooves of her sandals.

The memory of the landlady weaving her children's sweaters in the shade of a mulberry tree establishes her connection with Loom, twenty-eight years and thousands of miles later. She watches him every chance she gets: in the morning before leaving for the store, in the evening when she returns, and on days like this when a snowstorm keeps them indoors. At the store, she dreams about strolls in the park during working hours, when the risks of being seen are slim. Seen by whom, you silly old maid, she chides herself. She doesn't know anyone in town, and what does it matter? This habit she has of watching over her shoulder lest she's caught acting improperly, contemplating thoughts she shouldn't be contemplating at forty-four about a man she doesn't know.

Marie acts as her link to Loom when Josephine is at the store. She doesn't know where her niece finds the time, with a full load at the college and a part-time job at the flower shop. When Josephine returns in the evening, Marie half reports, half makes up what she has seen, her eyes glued to her aunt's face and taking her cues from her reactions, thrilled to see her spinster aunt finally interested in a man. Josephine pares down her excesses. She wants accuracy: the music he has been listening to, the progress he has made on the shed he has been building since before Thanksgiving.

"Why can't he leave well enough alone?" Marie asks, lighting up a new cigarette. She is careful not to be heard by her mother downstairs. Loom is still clearing his walkway, a picture of sober efficiency. Josephine marvels at his fortitude in braving a storm in progress. Her inclination is to wait the storm out, then dig only where absolutely needed, leaving to nature or chance the task of making passages.

Downstairs in the kitchen, Josephine's sister-in-law Salma is making a racket, banging pots and pans and calling on Marie to help with breakfast, which is her roundabout way of summoning Josephine. Marie makes a face before stubbing out her cigarette in the ashtray and running back to her room, her frequently shampooed hair leaving behind a scent of watermelon.

Standing at her window, watching Loom, waiting for Eva.

Maybe they can pick up where they left off. The snow deferring Eva's coming, allowing Josephine to prepare, to decide which dusty rooms to air out, which ones to keep bolted.

In the glass, she sees her face framed by her limp hair and beyond it the stooped figure of Loom inside a white wind. Winter has a way of giving the land back its wilderness. Perhaps it is the muffle and enigma of snow, of time slowing down. Maybe it is the dreams that make the land wild. Only the exterior is cool, old Loom. I made you a part of my dreams, the part where my looks do not matter.

No longer young, never attractive, unmarried, childless, a female peeping Tom, a slave to her brother's store and to his wife. Exultant, she opens the window and yells out, "Fine morning, Mr. Loom!" and to illustrate, she sticks out her tongue and tastes the icy fuzziness of winter. He can't hear her and she closes the window. At the door, she hears her mother's footfalls on the stairs and hesitates. She returns to sit on her bed and smoke one last cigarette, just this last one, before she must go down and face Salma.

HE PUSHES THE SHOVEL DOWN with one foot on the back of the blade and looks at the sky. Snowflakes swirling like moths to the light. Plenty of material for what he has in mind, a mountain of snow lifting from the front side of the driveway it will take him the better part of the day to build. He looks down and grips the handle of the shovel with his right hand and the lower part with his left. Swinging the shovel behind him then forward and down, he picks up half a shovelful at a clip. The snow is wet and heavy and flies with his forward swing, headed for the small mound he's managed to pile since he started at dawn. Some of the snow falls to the sides, and five loads is what he allows himself before he has to stop and tamp it down with the back of his shovel, smoothing it the way he's seen brick layers smooth cement between the blocks. The mound packs itself solid, scrunches and tightens and takes on the next load.

He runs the blade back and forth a few times over the same spot, as if to claim every last bit of fallen snow. He imagines Brendan squatting behind the mound and packing a snow ball. He sees himself hobbling slowly toward him, an easy target in his dark clothing, feigning outraged befuddlement when the ball hits him squarely in the chest, while Brendan, hooting and howling, "You're dead! You're soooo dead," is ducking for new ammunition. Ordinarily reluctant to grant his son an easy victory (for how else would he have hoped to toughen his shy and tenderhearted boy?), he would have felt perfectly justified after this last concession to bend down, pack a handful of snow, and pounce before his boy knew what hit him.

He woke up early this morning and went to work under the gray sky, hunkered over against the wind. He can hear the snow pelting the ground, the whisper of its tearing against the chicken wire fence around the vegetable garden. His quick breathing is the only human sound for miles. Breathing is what the snow reminds him of, with its quiet, even rhythm. Right now he needs this snow the way he needs oxygen.

A piece of the blacktop peels back with his next load, right where several cracks he noticed this past summer were beginning to appear. He'll go to the hardware store for some filler as soon as the storm lets up. He feels a headache creeping from the kinks in his neck and forking out to assault his temples. All he's managed after two hours of toiling is a pile no higher than his midriff. Yet Brendan would have understood. Would have jumped up and down in excitement, as if a bumpy, uneven pile of fresh snow was everything his little heart had ever desired.

The pounding in his head worsens. He stops to look at his watch and decides he's been toiling long enough to allow himself a short break. He props the shovel against the garage and walks over to the house. In the mud room, he gives his coat a few quick shakes before hanging it from a wooden hook on the wall, then neatly places his boots on the mat where they will drip heel next to heel, facing the yard for when he needs to go out again. In the kitchen he opens a cupboard. Plenty of hot chocolate, a few cans of bean soup, a half-eaten loaf of bread, a carton of cigarettes. He is more than ready for the storm. He reaches for a bottle of aspirin and swallows two tablets without water. In the living room, the fire is dying. He throws in yesterday's newspaper and a couple of logs, stoking it with a degree of fury, as if goading it to reach inside his head and ravish the pain, burn it down to a crisp and send him back outside where he should be, building an igloo, not here taking time off, when time is the last thing he should be allowed to have.

IT MUST BE NINETY DEGREES IN HERE. Mother, no doubt. As if by cranking up the heat she is expelling the cold and something worse besides. I kick away the sheets. Stupidly, I forgot to bum a few extra cigarettes from my aunt before I left her in her room to her daily ritual of Loom gazing.

Everyone's been acting strange—OK, stranger than usual—since my father's cousin announced her visit. All week my mother's been in a frenzy of cleaning, and now she's cross because the cousin's stuck in New York and we'll end up having to eat the leg of lamb for lunch; heaven forbid we should indulge unless there's company, which never happens anyway.

I've taken off my pajama bottoms and unbuttoned the top and tied it into a knot. I stretch out on the bed and prop myself up on one elbow, à la Elle McPherson who's staring back at me from her poster on the wall. Hair tossed back, breasts squeezed together to make them seem bigger than they really are. I pucker up and narrow my eyes. Then I remember. I go to the mirror and look at my belly, pressing down, kneading the muscles, feeling for a potential pulse. Kevin wore a condom. I am safe. I will go to Berkeley.

I fall down on the bed. It's too hot and there's nothing to do. My mother is calling me. "Marie, Marie," she yells in that voice I hate, half martyr and half mad despot. I get up and put Janis Joplin on, then lock the door and wait. It takes her a while to climb the stairs because of her bad knees, but here she is, as predictable as morning, knocking on my door and ordering me to turn that thing down. I oblige. Once again I have gotten a rise out of her. But it's not as fun as it used to be. I must be bored.

I am bored. Wretchedly, utterly, down to my pinky toes. My best friend Shirley is visiting her father in Florida. Kevin's in North Carolina spending Christmas with his grandparents. My only family is all under this one roof. You decide what's wrong with this picture.

I make up my mind to call Shirley's mom, on the unlikely chance that Shirley has decided to leave Florida earlier than planned. I don't believe this for a minute, but I tiptoe anyway to the hallway and hijack the cordless. In her scratchy voice, Mrs. Dougherty dashes my delicate hopes: Shirley will be back in the middle of January, as originally planned. Despite my disappointment I don't hang up. I like Shirley's mom, with her Seventies bouffant hair and her lumpy thighs she's not shy about showing off in the summer months and sometimes beyond. They're wiggly and crisscrossed with varicose veins, but she doesn't care. Veins like rivers snaking down the backs of those thighs you can almost feel throbbing under the skin, but she walks her dog Duncan every day at five o'clock on the dot, yanking that leash with sure authority every time Duncan gets feisty at the sight of a human or fellow canine. She and Shirley's dad have been divorced since Shirley was a toddler, which is why my dad doesn't like my best friend. I'm not sure what it is exactly he finds objectionable, the divorce itself or the absence of a lawful male to steer mother and daughter away from needless sin. Little does he know that, of the two of us, it's his little daughter who's no longer a virgin.

I've never seen Mrs. Dougherty with a man. If she has a boyfriend, she keeps him well hidden. I secretly hope she'll take me into her confidence one day, whisper her scandalous secrets in my ear while we sit on the stoop, throwing a stick to Duncan. But it's never happened, and I'm left to wonder what she does in her spare time besides not giving a rip what people think.

I inquire politely after her health, a question she knows to be the small empty talk it is and ignores. Instead she tells me that she's considering trading in her Camaro for a motorcycle but is hesitating because of her cottage in the mountains. She's not sure a motorcycle can make the trip in winter. "What do you think, Marie Darling?" She's been calling me Marie Darling since the day Shirley introduced us ten years ago. I like it. On the other hand, the habibti that my father and grandmother lavish on me (my mother doesn't bother with sweet nothings. Her love is practical and unadorned), makes me feel beholden.

I hear Mrs. Dougherty on the other end take a pull on her cigarette. I tell her that if a motorcycle is what she wants, she should go for it. I'm lying through my teeth. Shirley and I wouldn't know what to do with ourselves without the car her mother generously lends, no questions asked. When I hang up, I am feeling totally down. On the upside, with any luck, by this time next year I will have been gone a whole semester.

With Shirley I feel normal, like a fish in water. At the local diner where we party regularly, Shirley and I gladly accept free drinks (alcoholic when John is tending the bar and will allow you a dash in your spritzer if you don't exceed the limit of his forbearance), but the local male crop has long lost its appeal. Company is always plentiful in Scarabee where there is a shortage of women, most of whom skip town as soon as they know better. Why the men don't follow suit is anyone's guess. We cross and uncross our legs, the cracked leather of the seats digging into our thighs, and sneak out the back door the moment our company starts expecting something in return.

The other night Shirley parked the car on a hilltop. As usual, we had her mom's car because my dad refuses to lend his. He'd be sorry if he saw the way Shirley drives. She has something against using her brakes and says it's a form of self-denial, waiting until the last minute, when it's as plain as that nose on her face that it's the only way to avert disaster. In the meantime, I am clutching the dash and laughing till I am practically wetting my pants.

We could see Scarabee at the foot of the hill, a wide distance separating the houses, the lights scattered through the gentle valley the town sits on. Hypnotic, inviting, dangerously alluring, we said of Scarabee, conceding it might have some hidden charm, with its rolling hills and quaint streets the tourists like. A picture, we agreed, of domestic loveliness, before we swiftly hooked our pinkies and swore that the first one out of Sacarabee would not rest until she had rescued the other. A viper's nest, we said of our town. We described it in other vile terms without completely believing what we were saying. Finally admitted that perhaps all it was guilty of was (1) being boring and (2) housing our parents, while suspecting that (1) was probably the direct result of (2). In a moment of inspiration, I thought how one's life was made up of all these emotions: love, hate, boredom. One minute you're soaring, and the next you're crashing into total disgust. I can't make heads or tails of it.

I will be the first to leave. I know that as surely as I know my name. I want to go somewhere warm to study plants. Gardening is my passion. The yard is all my doing, the flower beds and the retaining wall and the sturdy lawn. I've been secretly applying to colleges and universities in California. My first choice is Berkeley. I see myself at a large university, hanging out with people from all over the world. To my parents, Scarabee is the world, and it is all they can do to figure it out.

I would love to have Shirley here right now, with her big hair and green fingernails, concocting some prank not everyone's bound to find funny. She's a bundle of contradictions, is a mild way of putting it. She's crazy about Marlon Brando in *The Last Tango in Paris* and wants to travel to France and fuck French men, or, at the very least, American men who have the allure and anguish of the French. In the same breath, she talks about marrying young and having a tribe of children. No steady boyfriend anywhere in the picture, though.

In the kitchen, my mother slams doors, bangs pans on the stove, and leaves the water running. I could swear she has replaced language with a steady rumble. I hear her cursing in Arabic. In the foul language department, my Arabic is fluent, but otherwise I stick to English.

The strange thing about my mother is that she is soft-spoken in public, her voice barely above a whisper. She sure makes up for it at home. That's what I hate about her. One thing at home and another in public, as if she's lying all the time, and I don't know what she's covering up.

I sneak back to the hallway and find what I am looking for in the linen closet. I empty out the plastic bag on my bed and thumb through the photos until I find two of Eva. I might as well pass the time investigating the woman responsible for all the commotion.

In the first picture, Eva is sitting outside under a green awning. She is wearing white shorts and a blue tank top, and seems to be about my age. She is tilted forward, with her hands on the arms of the chair as if she's getting ready to stand up. She is in the shade, except for her feet, which seem small for her frame. In the second picture, Eva is older, perhaps in her twenties. The room where she is sitting is furnished expensively. There is a large painting behind her and a potted plant on a claw-footed table. She is wearing a red dress and sandals. Her legs are long and tanned. She is laughing at something the woman sitting next to her is saying. Her hair is colored in a shade of light brown and doesn't suit her. She looks phony somehow—maybe she's laughing too hard—but also a little vulnerable, perhaps because of those small feet that seem out of keeping with the rest of her body.

As far as I know, Eva, who, if you believe my mother, slept with legions of men after her husband's death, is the only colorful character in my father's family, who comes from solid mountain stock. (My mother came right out and said it, about Eva. She's not an honest woman, she said. I pretended to be shocked but my mother wasn't fooled and sent me to my room. Her husband is—hello?—*dead*, I said before leaving. My mother wasn't happy with that. No reason, she said, to act like a whore.)

On my mother's side, my great-grandmother almost started a mutiny by eloping with a Turkish soldier, back when Lebanon was a small possession of the Ottoman Empire. This is how I got my auburn hair. It was my great-grandmother who performed the seduction, strutting to the coffee shop where he played backgammon with the locals, showing off a bit of ankle. Since the soldier was a Muslim, the family raised objections, forcing the lovers to elope. But having a son-in-law who could pull strings and provide cousins and uncles with employment and little gifts had definite advantages, and eventually the family came around, especially when he agreed to convert for the sake of his beloved.

I return the pictures to the linen closet, stopping by my aunt's room. No sound there. She must be sitting by the window watching Loom, an ashtray in one hand, her feet in old slippers. Teta Emilie is probably downstairs, bullied into the kitchen by my mother who can't stand to see people idling away the time. I return to my room and quietly shut the door. I put Janis Joplin back on and think of Kevin.

When I found the blood on my underwear my heart skipped a beat. Finally. I was a new person, un-Lebanese. But then I began to feel guilty. I had gone and left my parents behind. For a while, regret spoiled my joy.

EVA FIGHTS WITH HER HAND LUGGAGE. She looks in the dresser for a pair of scissors to cut through the zipper, and returns to the bed empty-handed. Stupid bag. She should have bought a new one before leaving Beirut. The zipper has been jamming since she purchased it from a store in Jounieh seven years earlier to go on a trip to Italy with a man she barely knew and discovered too late that she didn't really like. (Although he redeemed himself in the medieval northern town where they spent a fortnight, his burly looks suddenly poetic under the stone arches.) She wouldn't mind his company right now, in this hotel room thousands of miles from a single soul she knows and the blasted wind rattling the windowpanes.

She gives her full attention to the zipper, which yields enough for her hand to go crawling in and looking for the carton of cigarettes she bought at the airport. Ignoring the no smoking sign on the door, she lights up a cigarette. A few more tugs and the bag zips open. She lets out a sigh and retrieves underwear, a small mirror, tweezers, tampons, and a box of crackers, all of which were packed by Marietta, who has been her sturdy and dependable maid of ten years. Eva must not forget to buy gifts for Marietta's brothers and sisters in Sri Lanka.

Eva hates shopping but loves clothes. Her closet is full of signature items. Of course, there is always the possibility that the clothes were manufactured cheaply in some shop in Bourj Hammoud and sold as genuine articles. This is why Eva has lately started going to a boutique in Hamra where, according to her friend Amal whose authority on matters of fashion is irrefutable, everything, down to the frilly underwear and the belts with metal buckles the size of saucers, is made in Europe.

On TV, a young couple argues over a lasagna recipe in front of an invisible audience who laughs at jokes she doesn't get. She turns down the volume but continues to watch the attractive blond woman and her excitable husband waving wooden spoons at each other.

She might as well admit it: she is worried about the meeting with her family. She will be secretly criticized for her money-spending habits, her reputation with men (although she hasn't lived up to it lately, and is doubtful that she ever has), and, most of all, for having a maid. Her cousin Josephine will purse her lips every time Marietta's name comes up.

The tediousness of it! Eva turns off the TV and lies down on her back. Like Uncle Farid's lectures a long time ago, through which she'd sat enchanted with the rest of them, his beatific and mostly female audience listening to his every word, his wife and daughter (everything about Josephine smug and boastful: He is mine, my own father!), the nuns at school (although they would allow themselves only snippets, courting sin without abandoning themselves to it), his awed and pimpled students. A secular society. The elimination of confessionalism. A home for the Palestinians. He was thunderous, he was a beautiful fire that singed at the same time it tantalized. They had felt themselves lifted, buoyed up by his words to rise above the rest of the sorry world. Yet a nugget of disbelief began to form in her, a chink in her rock-solid faith she started cultivating out of sheer spite and the desire to be done with blind faith.

Is Marietta a Muslim? It has never occurred to Eva to find out. She has long since stopped going to church and assumes the same indifference to religion in someone sharing her quarters. Regardless, her maid is a gem. Eva demolishes the box of crackers, angry with herself. Why has it never occurred to her to ask? Josephine will surely want to know.

The blasted snow and her blasted family. It rankles her that, after all these years, she must still feel the need to defend herself.

"Vicious, vicious snow!" she gets up to yell and makes a fist at the weather. She has left a perfectly blue sky in Jounieh for this. It was her fault for choosing to come in the middle of December. She made her decision on a whim, one day realizing that her aunt Emilie and her cousins were the last close relatives she had in the world. Both her parents were dead, and she wasn't on talking terms with her deceased husband's family who blamed her for squandering his money.

On that same day, she looked in the mirror and saw her mother's crow's feet and her father's tendency for jowliness. It was one of two things: either corner the friend who had come back changed from a vacation in Bonn and squeeze from her the name of the plastic surgeon responsible for the transformation; or fly to the United States to spend Christmas with her only remaining family. Fearing the scalpel more than the prospect of a double chin, she looked in her closet, hoping to find there all she needed for the icy weather of North America without having to go shopping. She was a skier and had plenty of warm clothes. She went to her beach chalet, which in the winter she used for storage, and trembling with the cold of the unheated rooms, collected hats, gloves, and a ski jacket.

When she told them about her trip, her friends quickly approved, happy, she suspected, to be relieved for a while of the thankless task of trying to fix her up. She had a reputation for being hard to please. She, on the other hand, considered her fussiness perfectly justified. To punish her friends for meddling, she knocked down the men they produced for her one by one, like vanquished pieces on a chess board.

She didn't know what kind of men she preferred anymore. They all seemed alike. She couldn't remember the last time she had been with a man. It couldn't have been the friend she took to Italy on that unfortunate trip. If there were others after him they were in a blur now. She still missed Robert. She saw a movie once where the woman pickled her musician husband's fingers after he had died in a coal mine. She wished she'd had that presence of mind. But she would have had to keep Robert's entire head, for how could she have preserved his smile, the way his eyes softened when he looked at her? She would have still had to rely on her recollections.

She wasn't physically faithful to his memory. He had left her with enough money to dispense with conventions. But her affairs barely distracted her. For years, she would wake up in the middle of the night crying, convinced he'd come back and left while she was still sleeping.

When she got tired of men she started taking in stray cats. In one of her pictures, she is surrounded by eleven cats, perched on her shoulders, curled in her lap, hanging from her sides like extra limbs. No wonder she thought she would never be alone again. But she soon got bored with them, too, their standoffishness, the way she had to beg for attention, as if she was forcing them into affection. She was through with begging.

Her stomach grumbles. She hasn't eaten anything besides a few crackers since her last meal on the plane and decides to check out the restaurant. Before going out, she looks around. In the few hours she's been here she has managed to turn the room into a mess: soggy towels on the bathroom floor, the bed sheets tangled, her clothes strewn as if in the wake of a hurricane. She's a hopeless slob. No wonder she needs Marietta. Embarrassed, she considers hanging the "Do Not Disturb" sign on the door then decides against it. If everyone had her scruples, the maids of the world would be unemployed. Carmen, the hotel maid, has left her a note wishing her a pleasant stay, and Josephine rereads the note, touched once again by the neat handwriting. Reassured that slobs like herself exist to provide employment to the Carmens of the world, she quickly slips a full pack of cigarettes in her purse and heads out to the elevator, making a mental note to herself to call Josephine again after breakfast.

I HOLD IN MY HAND the dried fig my grandmother gave me when I became interested in gardening. "You can try planting the seeds," she said, "but they only grow in warm weather." At the time, I was convinced she was silently encouraging me to leave. I wrapped the fig in tissue and put it in a drawer under a heap of socks. Now, I wonder if she wasn't preparing herself for a lifetime without fig trees.

It wasn't the fig that caused my love of gardening. The fig was confirmation. It pleased me to know that my grandmother had noticed my busyness in the garden, that she believed I had meant every seed I planted and every stone I carefully arranged around the flower beds. She'd been a gardener, too, although not a serious one, she was quick to say, looking after her small plot outside her first-floor apartment in Beirut. But one could do so much more than putter about on a small piece of land. She wished me grand dreams.

All this she told me before she became almost mute. Her silence began three years ago. We didn't notice it until the day she declined without a word a second serving of stewed okra. She had never refused stewed okra before. We suddenly realized she hadn't spoken a word in weeks. Just like that, a dish of stewed okra turned down brought us to a revelation.

Although it happens more and more rarely, my grandmother will still talk to me when no one is around. Once in a while, she tells me to be nice to my mother. To which I always reply with my limited Arabic that my mother drives me crazy.

Speaking of crazy. My mother is again banging on my door. The way she can creep up the stairs without a sound infuriates me. I imagine the fleshy part of her arm jiggling as she pounds then stops to wait for an answer, fist at the ready. I briefly consider not answering, but my father would be up next and I am in no mood for a confrontation. I turn the music down and say that I will be right down. My mother's feet thud down the stairs. I throw a pillow against the wall. The silence presses beneath the music, echoing in the corners. No matter how hard I try to disguise it, the silence is the essence, the spirit of the house. Nothing can penetrate it, which makes me feel, as always when I am home, that I am trapped, cut off from normal living.

What I wouldn't do for a cigarette right now. I take a peek in my aunt's room, but it's empty and there is no sign of cigarettes anywhere. I scuffle back to my room and try not to bang the door. I swear I'll start screaming soon.

My father must be fussing with the thermostat again, setting it at sixty degrees, the limit of his economy. "The same temperature you set the air conditioner to when it's hot, isn't it? So what's the matter with it now?" he says when my mother starts complaining. "Oh, for a little breeze" he says in his best imitation of her, heaving a sigh and fanning his face with limp hands, which produces a blend of murderous rage and amused tolerance on my mother's face.

I am in bed, wrapped in the cover like a sausage. I look down at my feet raised on the footboard. My bedspread is a sorry Laura Ashley jungle of green vines on a white background with pink roses around the edges. The sheets are light blue, which gives the pleasant impression of being adrift at sea. Beyond my twitchy feet, there's a white Formica dresser my mother picked up at Wal-Mart. Next to it, a bookcase full of gardening magazines, the complete collection of Emily Dickinson's poems, a copy of *Chicken Soup for the Soul,* and all the novels of George Eliot and Jane Austen. The only window in the room has a curtain with the same pattern as the bedspread. On the left wall there is a Georgia O'Keefe poster and, on the right, the Elle McPherson poster next to a vanity.

I pull the cover over my head and stretch in the trapped warmth. The light diffused through the cover is cupped in a pool.

I miss the flower shop. My boss has been giving me more responsibility lately since the customers started asking for my services. I like to take unassuming flowers like Queen Anne's lace and surround them with low-growing plants like wood anemones. They look like delicate clouds over a teeming jungle. You don't need a lot of different flowers to make a good arrangement. No two flowers from the same genus are ever exactly alike. That's what I keep telling my aunt Josephine when she fusses with plants and mixes boxwood with euonymus, lilac, and forsythias and makes a mess of things.

I hate interruptions when I am in the middle of an arrangement. The other day Kevin started kissing my neck while I was putting together several bouquets for a Jehovah's Witness convention. I was particularly nervous because this was my first big job and I didn't know the first thing about Jehovah's Witnesses, except that they have demoted the Virgin Mary, which is a shame really considering she's the only female divinity with direct access to power.

"Can't you see I'm busy?" I snapped at him. He looked hurt. I tried apologizing, but he stormed out and I went back to my bleeding hearts and obedient plants, the whole thing softened with swirls of spring beauty. I thought the names alone would get the grade. Then I went out looking for Kevin and found him sulking in the garage. A few nice words and he was putty in my hands.

The temperature is back up again. Mother, who can't bear the cold, whose sensitive skin flakes and itches when she forgets to use a moisturizer. I don't remember the beauty she claims to have been, only a severe woman who constantly wrings her hands on a towel. I can still feel those hands when I was a child, picking me up under the arms and plunking me in the cold bathtub, then scrubbing me with a loofah. Serious about learning American ways, full of questions about the birthday parties I infrequently attended, yet never quite getting what that strange breed of people did do with their time.

Here is the story my mother likes to tell: I was conceived in Lebanon after a night of bombing. At daybreak, the sun came out for the first time in weeks and the fighting stopped. My mother will not ordinarily talk about such things but that was a special day because of the deal she'd made with God. In exchange for life in her womb, she promised to go to America. My father had been talking about leaving, but she had turned him down. She felt afraid of a world she could not imagine despite the subtitled American soap operas she watched on the rare nights they had electricity. She took this as an omen, the new world's elusiveness a premonition of future rejection. Four weeks after the bombing stopped, with me in her belly, they were on a plane to New York.

What was it like, back there? I ask my aunt, but her answers are brief, as if very little from that world has made it through the plane trip. My parents exaggerate and embellish the truth. Why did you leave, then? I ask them. They say that I am an insolent American girl and that they did not raise me to talk back. My father complains about raising a girl in America. He can't understand why I must work for strangers at the flower shop when I could be working for him. He returns home in the morning from the store, collapses on the sofa and fills the house with his snoring. When he wakes up, he expects coffee and milk on a tray, an empty bathroom to shave. My mother says he works all night, so where is the harm? Doesn't my aunt slave away at the store too, and still, my mother expects her to help.

My parents want me to marry a nice Lebanese boy who will settle nearby and make me many babies. No thanks.

I wonder why my aunt never married. Perhaps she left her country before she had time to fall in love. This morning I found her in her room looking at old Loom. I saw myself running to him and saying, "Mr. Loom, you have occupied our thoughts for the last few months. My aunt is crazy about you. Would you grant us the pleasure of your visit? You will find many unfamiliar things in our household, but I hope they will be pleasing. I hope you will not find us too strange, Mr. Loom."

In my world literature class, we study the old female poets of the world. My aunt could have been a Chinese poet of the antiquity, with her passions under control, her stripped-away dreams.

The teacher asked me to describe my heritage. I wrote about Jerusalem's King Solomon building his temple with the cedars of Lebanon, and the Phoenicians' cunning in the sea. I didn't deserve the A I got. I had merely copied the stories my mother read to me when I was a child. That teacher wrote a long comment praising my paper. I thought she had been too easily impressed.

I don't like that she has pegged me as someone far worldlier than her other students, even though I told her I was born in the next town and have never set foot outside the state. She says I have knowledge of the world, coming as I do from a home of immigrants. All I have is watered-down, secondhand knowledge, but I don't tell her that because I like getting A's. I don't even pronounce my last name right, my vowel sounds off, clipped where they should be long, rising and falling where they should stay flat. All I can say is that I would like for the Lebanese part to stop butting its nose into my American business.

IT IS ALREADY TEN. The mound is about equal to his height. When he climbs up the side to tamp down the uneven spots, he leaves deep footprints he fills in with new snow.

In the futility of this task lies his penance, yet he doesn't work any less diligently than he would if he expected Brendan to give him a sign. There will be no child squealing with pleasure to reward his labor. "Good job, Daddy." Brendan lying through his teeth when David would occasionally embark on a project for which he had no talent, would start assembling a piece of furniture or painting a wall because he imagined normal fathers across the land taking up hammer and brush on weekends and initiating little boys into manhood, a prelude of it at any rate. "You're doing a good job." Flitting from room to room and chattering nonstop, small for his age the first four years of his life, a growth spurt on the heel of his fifth birthday that settled his parents' fears about a life of unusually short stature.

He can feel the cold soothing him, clearing his head. He is a child of the north, born and raised in Buffalo where the hills are slick with snow a good part of the year. Years of working in New York City and living in the suburbs have not taken the country out of him. Since coming here, he has become reacquainted with a world of sounds: the clean split of the wood under the ax, the purr of the lawn mower, the chirping of crickets on summer nights so still one could almost hear, during intermissions, the leaves brushing against one another. He invites these sounds, coaxes them in one by one, standing in his yard, listening, peeling them apart.

Down he goes and comes back up, like a tireless human pendulum. He allows himself a short pause to gauge his progress. The round base about fourteen feet. The mound needs another foot at least in height. His fingers are numb. He takes off his gloves and slips his hands in his pockets to warm them, waiting a few minutes before putting on a dry pair of gloves he had slipped in his pocket before leaving the house.

When he was growing up, the snow sometimes came as early as October, bringing him to a state of peace, as if he himself were concealed under the mantel of white. Stand out and shine, his mother exhorted at home, and he fell short every new day. But in winter, he was neither better nor worse than the rest of God's creations, engulfed and exonerated by the snow that had overtaken the land, reducing variations in height to subtle gradations, blending the vivid colors of the warm months into a monochromatic plainness of white and gray. From this a limpid and cheerful blue sky would sometimes emerge, a temporary anomaly that did not threaten to overtake the most precious thing to him about winter, the quiet half-light in which he had been happiest. From the start, the snow has held him up.

Now, he is no longer a believer. Now, winter stands as a belated chance for reparation.

The wind seems to have picked up power and is pounding away at the house and howling at the icy air. He can barely feel his hands and goes back inside. The fire is still burning. The two tablets of aspirin he took earlier are still working. In the kitchen, he boils water for hot chocolate. He's always had a sweet tooth. The only change is the extra he allows himself now, the usual doses he used to get by on no longer enough.

He fills the electric kettle with water and plugs it in. It will be faster than the gas stove. He can't keep count of the cups of hot chocolate he drinks daily, or remember if he's had anything besides. He sits at the table to wait for the water to boil, his eyes wandering. The tablecloth frayed but clean. The dishes finished drying on the rack and ready to be stored away in the cupboard. The windows he will clean come spring. He looks up at the ceiling where the spiders have hung their webs since the last sweeping. His eyes travel down and rest on the tip of a tail emerging from behind a box of Wheaties on top of the microwave oven. He stands and picks up the little wooden statue. It's of Husky, their old dog, before cancer ravaged his stomach. Myra carved it in one day, her eyes following the dog as he darted after the ball Brendan threw. Fascinated, David watched as Husky took shape, the strong muscles under the sheen of his brown coat in that beautiful afternoon light slowly inhabiting the wood. He puts the little statue on the table and strokes the back as he would if Husky were here, his head on David's knee and his eyes closed to better enjoy the rub.

Perhaps Myra sent him the old woman. He smiles at the thought. This bit of solace he can take.

He was standing at his bedroom window when he saw her coming, her head bobbing behind the brush as if she were being carried by liquid. He grabbed his binoculars to take a close look. He had all but forgotten about other people. Had been giving his neighbors brief nods when it seemed outright rude to ignore their greetings.

She was birdlike and looked old, not so much in years, although she was that, too, but the kind of old he felt himself becoming, the best already behind him, each new day a miracle he'd gladly dispense with.

She put a plate on the top step, tucking in the edges of the paper towel, then hurried away and back into the brush.

He stayed at his window. He'd seen her leave and yet he hesitated to come down, as if she was playing a trick on him, lying in wait behind the bushes. He took his time coming down the stairs, annoyed by the revelation that he was still capable of being roused by passing mysteries.

On the plate he found fried chicken, two legs and half a breast arranged neatly under the paper towel and speckled with spices he didn't recognize immediately. (Later, he would remember the Middle Eastern medley, the cumin and allspice, the hint of nutmeg.) He brought the plate into the kitchen and put it on the table where it sat the whole afternoon before he finally threw the food away, washed and dried the plate, and left it on the kitchen counter for a few days before making up his mind to return it to her.

At first he thought of leaving a note to thank her for the food and ask her not to bother again. He would make up an excuse, a special diet he was on, doctor's orders, and leave it at that. But something about her had touched him, the way she treaded carefully on his narrow walkway, engulfed in tall boxwood, and her birdlike head, the small circumference of her flutterings. Without knowing why, he felt that she had taken a great risk for his sake.

He took the plate to the clearing and left it on a flat stone along with a small wooden angel, one of Myra's first creations, the wings unfolded, the feet poised for landing.

Their exchange lasted nearly two months. He would find a plate on his step, always covered and arranged with great care. He never ate the food, but washed the plate and left her one of Myra's statues all the same.

Gradually, he came to recognize the dishes. He'd eaten regularly at a Middle Eastern restaurant during his college days, the inexpensive falafel sandwiches filling his stomach without leaving a dent in his wallet. Yet he still wouldn't eat the older woman's food. Whoever was behind this, either his dead wife or the old woman acting on her own behalf for God knew what reason, would have to contend with his determination to be shielded from consolation. He gave the old woman Myra's statues one by one. Then one day he stopped leaving them and she stopped coming.

Myra would have liked this, her statues gifts for food. She began carving statues when Brendan started kindergarten and suddenly she had time on her hands. A bright flash brings her memory back, of her chiseling the wood, her face taut with concentration, the shavings curling from the knife like ribbon. Myra would have incited him to eat. He was happier with his diet of fast food, its honest, impersonal anonymity putting him in his place, mocking his illusions once of believing himself destined to great happiness.

The kettle whistles. He takes a packet of powdered chocolate from the cupboard, the kind with marshmallows, and tears it open. He pours the hot water from the kettle too quickly, spilling it on his hand. He swallows back a curse and cleans up the mess with a paper towel. His hand is red and he feels a blister coming. In the bathroom, he squeezes toothpaste from the tube and spreads a thin layer on his skin. The coolness instantly works its magic and the pain stops. Back in the living room, he sits by the fire. He'll have to allow the toothpaste to dry before he can put on his gloves. He turns on the TV and surfs the channels before settling on a chewing gum commercial. His left foot taps in time with the jingle. He stretches his legs and folds his hands over his chest, staring at the screen where the images flicker hazily in the daylight and make leaping shadows on the wall.

Suddenly he is beset by fear. He imagines the mound destroyed by the wind, smashed by some malevolence. In no time, he is back in the bathroom, knocking the contents of the medicine cabinet aside until he finds the gauze and wraps it around his hand, securing the seam with cloth tape. He picks up his coat and gloves on the way out without bothering to put them on.

The wind is coming in gusts against the house. Yet the mound waits, steadfast and patient, and David, exhausted by his long morning of labor and his panic at the prospect of being, once again, bereft, worn out but deeply relieved, falls to the ground and waits for he doesn't know what, sure nevertheless that something, right here and now in this harsh land and on this miserable morning, something requires his vigilant care.

IN EMILIE'S DAYS, young women cared about their appearance, the preening and primping as much a sign of thoughtfulness as of vanity. Taking the trouble is what it amounted to. Not loafing around in your grunge all day, as if you didn't owe the world something a little pleasanter to contemplate.

The two other figures in the kitchen assail her vision. Her daughter Josephine is sitting across the table in faded pajamas and greasy hair, sipping coffee and tracing the rim of the cup with her finger. Smoothly. Deliberately. She will not be rushed. No ma'am. She will not gush with offerings the way a guest might to lighten her stay by offering a hand, but will help when and if it suits her. Then there is her daughter-in-law baking mana'eesh while making sure to keep her back to Josephine and Emilie, the whole thing performed in a frightful dress that paints her face a cadaverous gray, as if she got up this morning and fixed herself up to go to her own funeral. "Your mother has an immense capacity for sulking," Emilie once heard Salma say to George. Emilie imagined her son shrugging, like sulking was woman's business he'd rather not get into.

At eighteen, Salma was a lovely bride, her cheeks round and smooth like risen dough. The day they set foot on this land, Salma's lovely plumpness slipped away from her cheeks and collected on her hips and chest and, there, proliferated. Before long she was looking like two different people, with her slender face and neck sitting on a body that seemed to have grown huge overnight. And now, at thirty-six, she looks at least ten years older. Emilie's heart breaks for her daughter-in-law, but there's no convincing the younger woman that the world bears her no ill. She's locked herself inside that head of hers, imagining the worst, and there's nothing or nobody who can talk her into coming out once in a while and seeing things like they truly are, sweet and sour, sometimes the sweetness taking over, and other times the sourness.

As headstrong as that granddaughter of hers who's locked herself in her room and has been blasting that awful music all morning. A good thing George is in the shower and hears nothing but the water and his own off-key singing, because you'd be able to hear him from the bottom of the hill when he starts hollering. Emilie doesn't interfere with the way these two raise their daughter, but there are times when she has to bite her tongue, seeing how they insist on treating this child as if they never boarded the plane eighteen years ago and came to this country for better or worse. No boys and ridiculous curfews and scrutinizing her friends until none can pass the test, and the ones who are still hanging around after that she must see in secret, as if it is a sin to be born poor or be making low grades or be the child of divorced parents. Seems to Emilie that once she could reason with her grandchild, but now that girl is itching to spread her wings and she'll be gone before you can say where. Emilie doesn't understand the new rules, but that's no reason not to try. Her son and daughter-in-law came here a long time ago and locked themselves in like the world outside was full of thorns. She knows all about thorns and what hurt feels like, and this can't be any more or any less than what she's seen before. Although she's not exactly a hero herself, a mute practically the last three years. A certain lethargy has taken over her jaw, as if she can no longer spare the energy for the intricacy of speech, the clamping together of thought and words. She has lost her nerve, minds her speech the way she minds the hard-to-find cardamom she uses to spice up her Turkish coffee. She is no longer sure of her knowledge, each word a perilous crossing into a world that sometimes seems no less castigating to her than it does to her daughter-in-law.

"The snow will be over by tomorrow morning and Eva will be here," Josephine says.

Emilie pats her daughter's hand. She can see that Josephine is worried, which is why Emilie can't bring herself to tell her daughter what's on her mind. How, for example, a part of her doesn't want tomorrow to come, while the other part can't wait.

She catches a glimpse of their neighbor through the sliding door. Her eyesight is strong enough to see the snow mound he has started. This young man's toiling makes him her companion. One night he sat straddling a tree stump in his back yard. She brought him a plate of fried chicken the next day, and, in her hurry to come back, she trampled the lettuce. A few days later she found the clean plate in the clearing, a wooden angel by its side.

All day her head spun as if she'd gone on and fallen in love, although she knew this wasn't it at all. Suddenly, she had an acute awareness of being alive, as if Farid had returned to take her dancing on Fridays again. She would spin and bend in her husband's arms, her feet barely touching the floor, giddy with the admiration the two of them were exciting in the other dancers. (The reckless lightness of those days, before. Before the war, before Farid's death, and mostly, before she had discovered Yussef. She would never feel that way again.) Now as then, vanity partly lay behind her excitement. She hid her neighbor's gifts in secret places, thrilled at having been singled out, and couldn't wait to bring him more food.

The day after her escapade in the lettuce patch, she served herself a large portion of stewed okra and rice and ate it on the back porch. The radio played in Marie's room, and she sat eating happily and listening to the music, and remembered how she would sit on her balcony over the sea and watch the gulls chase, swoop down at the azure sea then soar into the sunlit sky. She too would hear the call and go off wandering the streets of the city, recklessly (for eventually the war would start, and she would forget to tell her children of her whereabouts, and would neglect to take an umbrella on rainy days). She would walk sometimes for hours with the confident purpose of someone who knew where she was going and for whom the city held no secrets. When the bombs started falling, she took shelter where she found it and came out when calm returned, hugging the walls through the deserted streets. The next day, she would be off again, certain that something big and worthwhile lay in wait for her.

She must have anticipated her future exile, her loneliness in a foreign land whose strange streets did not invite her to strike out for new territories and lead her home when she tired of walking. How else can she justify the recklessness of those days in Beirut, the way she couldn't wait to be outside? Her trip into her neighbor's yard with a plate of fried chicken was the first time she had ventured out by herself in eighteen years.

A few days later she left him a bowl of rolled grape leaves. Again she sneaked out of the house at night and returned quickly, this time mindful of the lettuce. She wondered if he liked the lamb shanks that Salma had boiled with the leaves. The next morning she found the empty bowl on the front step with another wooden statue, a boy this time, slim and long, his shirt untucked, one leg extended as if he'd been captured while taking a walk. She marveled at the looseness he conveyed, motion and fluidity preserved in wood. After that she started leaving him food regularly. She liked receiving the small ornaments he left with the empty dishes. They were unpainted, but the carving was delicate and pure. She has nearly filled a shoe box with her little boys, peasant women, angels, eggs, and maple leaves. Each day she tried guessing what his next gift would be. How much she would have preferred to cook his meals with her own hands. She would have made him stewed chicken and grilled snapper, and once in a while she would have baked him a cake. But her daughter-in-law keeps a tight watch, so what she gave him was the making of another. Yet in the risk she took stealing out to his house to take him food, she took solace.

He gave her a wooden egg in exchange for roasted chicken, and another for fried okra. She can tell them apart because the second egg is from a darker wood, oak or birch, and is rougher on one side. The first one was carved from yellow pine. She put it on her windowsill where it catches the light. She keeps at least one at all time in the pocket of her housedress.

The eggs were lovely, pure and even, as if it had taken all his concentration to carve the long spherical lines, the meeting at both ends. Yet it must have been far more difficult to navigate the lines of a wooden angel. In the eggs, she saw, as much as the promise of new life, a shutting down, a withholding.

Then one day she received nothing for fried spinach and stewed beans. Since then she has not left him any food. He must have tired of their little game. It broke her heart.

You spend a lifetime in a place and you think you end up knowing it a little. But how do you know anything when you're cooped up inside the house counting the hours for the sun to set so you can finally retreat to your room and not bother staying on your best behavior; then, once night has fallen, counting the hours till the light shines again so you can have some company. Though eighteen years hardly qualifies as a lifetime given the span of years she has lived—and, from the look of things, she might still have to live, God, if there is one, help her.

Eighteen years already this last August, and still none of it hard solid. Salma was so pretty you couldn't help staring. Josephine was sprightly and dressed more carefully, and George was leaner and less officious. And Emilie. Back then, her hair was black and thick, and once in a while, she undid her bun and let it fall in waves down her back.

Eighteen years ago, she got ready to leave. There were dates and green almonds on the carts of the peddlers across the street, and the air was heavy with the heat. Till the last minute she was of two minds: to leave with her children or stay. George was firm. "Mother, you must come," he said. Josephine, too, wanted to stay, but later she changed her mind. By then the gardenias were blooming. Emilie would have liked to stay for the duration of their flowering, but they were scheduled to leave that same week. It was just as well, for she would hold on to the memory of their lovely white blossoms peeking out between the glossy leaves.

Every once in a while, the plane shook. The clouds below them were thick, drifting slowly like the white mist that hung over the river the week before their departure. Sometimes a wing disappeared inside a cloud, and she was afraid that it would never emerge, that they might start losing pieces of the plane, then plunge into the vastness.

She had imagined the plane piercing the sky, the different stages of their journey marked by shifts in color and texture. But they glided at first through an even blue sky, only vaguely aware that they had left land. Not until the plane flew over the clouds did they realize that they were moving. In a bare sky, nothing registered their passing.

They were in the air a long time before they arrived in New York. She remembers a long journey in the car before coming to Scarabee. The early years are all in a haze now. Her most solid memory is still that of flying. Even after they landed, she was still leaving.

George's original plan was to continue to Canada. He drove the rental car into a busy street that looped like a child's set of tiered car tracks then forked in several directions. He had instructed Josephine to look for signs to the north. She kept her eyes on the road, the big sister coming through for her brother like she always does in the end, a rivalry running deep between those two but banding together when it counts. The highway unrolled in strips flanked by lush greenery that looked well taken care of. This was more foliage than she had ever seen in Lebanon, but still the concrete dominated, a silver hard marrow twisting through the vegetation, as if it were the green that had encroached on the native landscape of tar and cement. They drove for a long time until it seemed that they would never reach Canada. The mountains loomed in the distance, unattainable. Sometimes they saw a sprinkling of houses in a large field. These were so small and few, and the land seemed so sparsely populated, that she settled meekly in the back seat, feeling small and insignificant.

They were turned down by the Canadians and drove back through Vermont. She doesn't exactly remember how they found Scarabee. Their settling here was almost a random act, as if they'd exhausted their ability to make decisions and allowed chance to lead them.

Scarabee seemed as good a place as any. She can't say she has been unhappy here.

Do you remember, dearest Eva, sitting on your balcony overlooking the Mediterranean and discussing happiness under a white awning? For me, happiness mattered less than faith. Not in God, an option for the faint-hearted, but in an unbreakable human connectedness. Happiness, you said, was a crystal bead you had once swallowed. It came from your mother's rosary, which broke one day and splashed its beads across the terrazzo tiles. You helped your mother put the rosary back together, and on impulse, placed one bead in your mouth to taste the exploding light and swallowed it by accident. You felt it for weeks afterward, lodged in your stomach, a comforting hardness in the slippery unknown of your body. We weren't that different in our definitions of happiness, looking for certainties through the muddle that enveloped our lives after the war, scooping hard tokens to stash away until such madness had faded. For you, a bead. For me, something less tangible but still secure, as tough and binding as the nylon filament stringing your mother's rosary. Family, my love, is what I mean. It was family that kept us sane when the war broke out, when the earth somersaulted and our lives with it. Josephine doesn't agree with me. She thinks the Americans have got it right. They are free, she says, they do as they please. When family tightens the noose they break away. To where, I wonder.

Don't go thinking I never gave it a thought. I went off roaming the streets, not sure what I was looking for but searching anyway. The clear blue of the sky and the sea pulling. We were so crowded on land that the only places you could escape to were the sky and the sea. So in reality there was nowhere to go. Funny how freedom is bound by geography. How it isn't an abstraction, not a prize in the sky you leap and snatch whole and stretch like royalty within its boundlessness. Still, break away to where? The same stories pursuing you or you pursuing them, you chasing after your tail all the same here or there. Then again, Eva, for all my wandering, maybe I didn't really give freedom a chance. And now, at sixty-nine, freedom still taunts me. I stay awake at night thinking of Farid and Yussef, and of you, more so lately, now that you are coming. And when I go to sleep, I dream of my hand poised to touch—whose shoulder, whose hovering arm?

She brushes a crumb off her skirt and straightens her back against the chair.

Her family came from the mountains. Her father was a landowner and the mukhtar, the chosen, their village leader. He was the maker and keeper of official documents, birth certificates and marriage records, sale deeds and wills, and he could list the history of any family with claims to a respectably long stay in their town. In dealing with newcomers, he would pull out their documents and politely point to the fact that the stack had grown since the last time. Her own family's roots spanned hundreds of years, their paper history packed in numerous metal boxes and frequently perused, she knew, by her father.

Their land was big. Through the summer months, they kept walnuts on the balcony and huge crates of apples in the cellar. Apples fell from the trees and lay on the ground, releasing their sweet rottenness into the breeze. It was possible to get slightly intoxicated on that smell when the sun was particularly hot and no one was there to see her lying next to a heap of fermenting apples and taking breath after deep breath.

And there was her sister Shirin, Eva's mother. Shirin's hair went gray years before hers, even though they were born only ten months apart, practically twins romping in that small hole of sun-scorched land they called home. Shooting up tall and strong, and nobody minding them until they started to draw male notice, and Mother rushed to her Singer, a frown knotting her forehead and needles dangerously sticking from her pursed lips, to produce for them skirts long enough to ward off temptation.

In her early twenties, Shirin started the fashion of drawing her hair back into a tight knot that pulled her skin taut around her face and gave her a look of vacant serenity. Emilie worried that her sister was in pain underneath her placid exterior. Also around this period, Shirin's frequent praying and rapid blinking began, as if reality was too big or unbending to be taken in all at once. She fingered her rosary while praying breathlessly. Keeping time with her gushing lips, her fingers would dart at the pictures of the saints hanging on the walls, brush the lower corner, then flutter to her lips where a kiss tossed lightly would send them again flying to the next picture. Saint Anthony isn't going anywhere, Emilie teased. She was puzzled by her sister. She knew Shirin didn't pray this fast to get it out of the way and get on with pleasanter things. (In Emilie's opinion, there was heaps of loveliness to be had: plucking sour grapes from the vine and eating them dipped in salt in the attic near a window with a view to the mountain where sheep bleated intermittently; the walnut tree in the shade of which they took heavenly naps.) No, Shirin loved praying. In everything else, her sister was slow and measured, but in prayer her soul soared. Afterward she would smile at Emilie, taking all the joking gracefully. You are so silly, she would say goodheartedly. They were inseparable, cooking each other little meals, efficiently dividing up the housework, agreeing about everything except the church and God, for whom Emilie saw no use at all.

Before she knew it, childhood was over and she was a grown woman with an eye for the town's high school history teacher. She and Farid conducted their silent courtship for months. She was the daughter of the mukhtar and could have had her pick of suitors, but she was interested only in Farid with his blue eyes and soft hair that flopped over his forehead. When he asked her father for her hand, her yes rang clearly through their high-ceilinged living room.

She ended up marrying before Shirin. Mysteriously landing herself a great catch, though someone without immediate kin to plead with him to reconsider this bride-to-be. For she had a reputation of being headstrong, and this made her, despite her father's stature, a dubious catch.

She was grateful that Farid was not a farmer. Although she loved the land, it had aged her father beyond his years. She also admired learning. She had had to quit school early, her parents unable to see a purpose for educating a girl beyond the primary level.

In the summer she turned twenty, she married Farid. Their wedding was an elaborate affair. Banquet tables were set outside. She remembers the cicadas singing, the smell of wild thyme and laurel, the roasted lamb shining with grease in the middle of each table, the rice with nuts and dates, the salads, the tabbouleh with hearts of lettuce sticking from the bowl like petals, the stewed zucchini and rolled grape leaves. She can still see the white tablecloths fluttering in the breeze and, to the side, their house, a crack snaking through the concrete, the water spots spreading like shadows in a painting. Their house was built at the edge of the town, on the top of a hill. Vegetation covered the hill all the way down to the church where they had celebrated her wedding.

In those days, she secretly loved this proximity to the church. She loved the pure music of the bells and their doleful rhythm when they announced a death. The church was the heart of the town. Emilie danced to the music of the tambourines and flutes, dizzy from too much arak. Once in a while, she would stop to think of all she was leaving behind, her life, her parents, and, most of all, Shirin. She went to her bedroom and buried her face in the bedsheets. Outside, the party was still going full tilt, and her mother was ululating. Someone improvised a poem, and Shirin came to get her. Twirling, the two sisters joined the crowd just as the poet was stepping off his makeshift podium. Glasses were raised to toast the newlyweds and someone showered her and Farid with rice.

Her parents were crazy about Farid. Although he wasn't a landowner, he had won them over with his sweet temper and eloquence. Yet he had kept from them his plan to live in Beirut after the wedding. He was born in the city and had moved to their town a few years after the death of his parents. Now, he told her, he was ready to go back. She remembers sitting on the edge of the bed the night of their wedding, rigid with anger. Who was this man she had tied her life to, who had kept his intentions secret until their wedding night, when she would have no choice but to follow him? Farid pleaded his case, but she was too angry to listen carefully. What she made out of his explanation amounted to this: He had learned the month before that he had been hired to teach history and civics at a private school in the city. Fearing her reaction, he had said nothing. He wanted her more than he could say, but he also couldn't wait to get out. By the end of the night, she let him hold her hand. The next day, she told her shocked parents. It was months before they forgave him.

In Beirut, they moved into a three-story building. The balconies in the back had a clear view to the sea. Back then, before the oil refineries had been built, you could still walk on the beach without stepping into puddles of oil. Before long the bulldozers came. The new buildings were painted a creamy white and the railings on the balconies blue. By the time Josephine was born, the neighborhood had filled with buildings and businesses. There was a car dealership next to their building, and on the first floor a shop sold farming equipment.

In Beirut, the food was not as fresh as she was accustomed to, and flowers sprung randomly in the greenless city. She grew pots of parsley and mint, begonias and geraniums, and missed her mountain. Although hired workers had done the hard labor, she had always helped with the harvest, barefooted in the fields. Now all she had was a balcony with a few pots. A few years later, they would move into a first-floor apartment with a small plot in the back, and there she would have a thriving vegetable and flower garden.

Beirut was hot and damp in the summer, and most people went to the mountains to escape the heat. Every June, when school broke up, she and Farid returned to the town. She couldn't wait to be outside roaming the fields and the orchards, returning at night with Shirin, their cheeks red like apples and their laughter filling the big house. Sometimes they had to interrupt their vacation and return to Beirut for a week or two while Farid met with the administrators at his school. Emilie would wander in their apartment like a lost soul, trying desperately to find a cool spot. There were none of the gentle breezes of her mountain except at night, when she and Farid would eat their dinner on the balcony next to the broad leaves of a potted palm.

After five years of marriage, she had still not borne him children. She wasn't in any hurry to get pregnant, but the days seemed endless with Farid at school.

It wasn't until Shirin, finally married, had moved to Beirut and gotten pregnant that Emilie followed suit. The sisters' bellies swelled in synchrony, Eva emerging first, Josephine following two weeks later, taking her sweet time, that girl, and using up the better part of three days and nights to show her little face. No wonder Emilie waited three full years before giving her a brother, and this time, with the bedsheet stuffed in her mouth to muffle her screams, she catapulted George out with a speed the doctor attending the birth claimed he had not witnessed before.

Eva and Josephine shared the same bed when Shirin came to visit. People often mistook them for twins. George grew up trying to insinuate himself in their friendship and, failing, affecting an indifferent contempt.

After two decades of teaching, Farid's ambition was to succeed the school's director who was retiring. But one day he was hit by a truck while coming home from work, and Emilie was left with two teenage children and a small pension. That same year Shirin died from brain cancer and the war started. It would go on for many years. Through it Emilie's children would graduate from school and find jobs, and her son would marry and decide to come to the United States. Through it she would help raise Eva as if she were her own. On still nights, while the city rested from the fighting, Emilie took stock of her losses. Everything reminded her of her husband and her sister: the fans that Farid had bought for every room in the apartment because he couldn't bear the summer heat; the brown chair where he liked to sit and read; his side of the closet, which would take her years to empty and which she would never use again; the seashell picture frame that Shirin had bought during a trip to the cedars; her rosaries and the pictures of her saints that Emilie couldn't bring herself to give away. The world she knew had come to an end. She held on to her keepsakes until she had to leave. They would not, she feared, survive the journey. She packed them in a trunk she gave to Eva. In the same trunk she put the incomplete deck of cards Yussef had once given her, one of the many small and useless gifts he would slip in her hand while she prepared to leave, his poor mind searching for a concrete reminder of her visit to guarantee she would not forget him once she was back in her world.

She stands up. To Josephine who asks, she replies that she has decided to wait for Eva's call in the living room. She feels Salma's eyes on her back as she crosses the hallway that separates the living room from the kitchen. She sits on the couch, well within view so that Salma can keep an eye on her through the French doors and make sure she's not bringing down the room or soiling the furniture.

She smoothes her dress and fidgets with the hem.

She will wait right here for the phone to ring.

GEORGE OPENS THE WINDOW to let out the steam, and shuts it quickly when the cold wind storms in through the screen with a volley of sharp ice pellets he receives smack in the chest. He returns to the mirror and wipes the fog off with a towel. Squirting a knoll of shaving foam into the palm of his hand, he spreads it over his lower face and neck. Then he rinses his fingers and makes a clean line where his mouth is. His lips appear pink and fleshy between the soft peaks of the cream, like something crawling timidly out of a hole. The face staring back at him looks surprised, as if slightly unsettled by what he sees: the balding head and flabby cheeks, the way his body slopes downward and away from his narrow shoulders to widths the mirror is too small to contain. Ordinarily his expression is placid at the time of the day when he shaves, the blade smoothly sinking in the foam and skiing expertly down the slopes of his face while his mind races ahead to all the things he must attend to. Ordinarily, he doesn't much care about the way he looks, derives even a certain pride from his bulk, which, he feels, is the outward manifestation of his position in life, one of prominence and achievement. For he tore up roots and brought his family to a new country and gave them a life as good as a man can provide. He has also taken care of his mother and sister for years. No man worth his salt would have left two women behind to fend for themselves. Not once did he regret his decision, although it made life hard, for his wife has never become accustomed to sharing her house with in-laws. He has done the right thing, and he has every reason to be proud of himself.

Ordinarily, he forgives himself the extra pounds he's piled on the last several years and accepts it as a man's prerogative to indulge on rich meals when he toils hard so that his family may live in prosperity. It's the nature of this country, all work and sweat, and barely enough time to enjoy the fruits of his labor. Some day soon he'll retire and spend his days leisurely fixing up the garage and who knows, maybe even building an addition in the back. Wouldn't it be nice to see three o'clock come and go without getting in the car and driving off to the store when normal folks are returning home to their families, knowing there's nothing to look forward to but the long solitary nights while he wonders why he bothers to stay open, the only people out on the street at that hour stopping at the pump without coming inside, when everybody knows there's no money to be made in gas when you're a small store owner.

This goes on until the truckers start coming in the early morning hours for fuel and for the fresh coffee he's got ready and waiting, and the sticky buns and apple strudels the guy from Freihauffer delivers every morning at 4 a.m. on the dot. George refills their coffee for free and heats up their pastries in the microwave and takes care of them as good as their own mamas. He knows the regulars and makes it a point to remember the names of their wives and children. His favorite is Lucas, a big man of about fifty who's been coming the last ten years and never fails to ask him about back home. He sticks around until the paper gets delivered, he and George watching while the delivery man comes in without a good morning or hello and drops his bundle on the floor and leaves in a hurry, his truck idling outside and stinking up the morning air. George cuts the yellow twine with his penknife and hands Lucas the top copy, hot off the press, he likes to say, and Lucas drops his coins on the counter and takes his second cup of coffee and sticky bun to the bench outside when it's warm or to a chair in the corner otherwise, and starts reading. In the meantime George knows enough to stay out of his way until he's finished, at which point Lucas stands up and walks to the bathroom in the back to rinse his hands, then says goodbye and walks out.

George is usually disappointed that Lucas won't make mention of the news he's just finished reading, and he promises himself to store some tidbits in his head to share with his friend the next morning. But he usually gets busy tending to customers and tidying up, and he forgets to read the paper until it's eight and time to go home and Josephine is there to relieve him and the news is stale and he's too beat to care. Yes, he loves it when the truckers come. It feels good to see his register fill up with cash and to know that he'll have enough for creditors and then some for personal enjoyment. But what he really loves is knowing that these truckers like him and keep coming back and bestowing on his life habit and tradition.

Usually, he's pretty happy with his lot. Something happens every now and then to cloud up his mood, but he's got only himself to blame for what happened the other day. Went looking for those pictures in the attic, although told himself he was really looking for the two-by-fours he had left there the year before, thinking he might start building that box Salma has had her heart set on since they moved to this house, a nice big box to store pillows and blankets and maybe even their winter clothes and double up as a sitting bench in the basement. He knew he didn't just happen on those old photos of himself, looking young and slim and with just a hint of the spread to come. When he went rummaging in the old trunk for pictures from back home, he was hoping to find Eva in them. She was always spending time at their apartment. It must have been lonely at her place, with his aunt obsessed with her prayers and his aunt's husband getting drunk when he wasn't fixing cars.

Sure enough, there she was, standing on their verandah in the full sun, with his mother's potted plants behind her. In another picture, she is at the dinner table with a cigarette in her hand, her lovely hair streaming down. In a black-and-white photo, she is watering the garden. In the background, he can see his father reading the paper.

He sat in the attic staring at the photos. A familiar jitteriness crept up on him, and he pushed it back. He hadn't thought of her all these years, and wasn't it the most natural thing in the world to want to catch up with your own cousin, your flesh and blood? He'd have preferred not to have to see her again, but that's neither here nor there. She'll be coming soon, and if it weren't for this blasted storm she'd be here right now sharing their breakfast and regaling them with her stories and making everyone misty-eyed and awkward. And he'll be feeling foolish again in her presence, like he would never be in her league no matter how high he rose in life or how wide his flesh spread.

He rinses the razor and taps it against the sink. He twists his mouth to the side to give the blade a smooth surface and attacks the second half of his face. He is careful, especially around the narrow terrain of chin and dimple where he seems to get in trouble, sometimes sinking in the crease too fast, or, on the contrary, forgetting it altogether and passing over in one clean sweep and slicing off a bit of skin. His face, with its complicated curves, is unforgiving. But it reminds him that he must concentrate and take his time, which he is prone to doing anyway; for he sees the wisdom of unhurried action. Besides, he hates blood. There are times, when he is in a hurry, or when he is particularly preoccupied, when he emerges with numerous nicks he stanches with toilet paper. He's gone to work like this before, his face speckled with toilet paper, and had the distinct impression that this sight had disturbed his customers.

He'll have to speak to Eva eventually. He wonders how in the world he'll be able to face her again after what happened. After the unfortunate business of having a crush on her, briefly, and then, foolishly, telling her and being rejected. He's not sure what he'll say. Maybe they'll talk about the situation in Lebanon. She's always been savvy when it came to politics, remembering names and dates, seeing the hidden strings everyone missed. He stops his mind from wandering off to her alleged affairs after Robert died. There might be some truth behind the rumors, he doesn't discount the possibility, she is a grown woman and George is no fool. A woman is as headstrong as a man and will follow her own course, and there's nothing anyone can do about it.

He considers himself wise, although he married young and has spent the better part of his life working and never experienced youth the way of normal people, with all the dating and carefree meandering and exploring until you got that smelling the roses business out of your system and declared yourself ready for something more stable.

But, he sighs, he is not wise enough when it comes to his own daughter, who can cause him to lose his temper like no one he knows. George won't often admit this to himself, but sometimes he regrets his decision to drag his family here to this, yes, he will say it, God-forsaken country, the best country in the world but, where it counts, as godless and arid as the barest desert. It was his decision and he will take responsibility for it, but if they'd stayed home maybe things would have turned out differently, at least where his daughter is concerned. George doesn't like defeat or self-pity, but he wonders whether things would have been simpler back home. Yet nothing is ever simple. Things don't fall neatly in place just because you're home. He'll have to remember this the next time the thought of home tugs at his heart.

Still, there's something to be said for staying in the country of one's birth. He has lost his place in the world. Once in a while he feels sure-footed, but this clarity evaporates the moment he's out the door. This land still intimidates him after all the years he's lived here. His customers, except for the truckers, good men and women all of them, still fickle, still asking him if George is his real name, as if waiting for the day when he will finally confess to being named Ali or Ahmed, and still bringing up those damned camels. The best thing about retiring will be staying home and working on building benches for Salma and that screened porch she's been wanting for years.

He hears the phone ring. Yes, Eva is a grown woman. He taps the razor blade one last time against the sink and turns off the water. He has better things to think about. Like, for example, how to bring business during the dead time between midnight and three in the morning before the truckers start coming in. These are the productive thoughts he must entertain instead. He must resist the trivial course his mind takes occasionally, living as he does in a house full of females.

He thinks about the loss he is incurring right now between the sandwiches on consignment and the food his mother and Salma prepare every day (the grape leaves, the kibbi—it makes him proud to think that he has introduced this food to his customers, it makes him hold his head up high), and which will have to be thrown away. He figures a setback of four hundred dollars. More than a few days' profit. It isn't much, but George hates waste. Hates this last contrariness of nature, as if it's out to ruin him. He's being foolish and it irritates him, because at his age he should have more sense than to imagine deliberate conniving behind the random acts of nature. He tries to find the good in all this. He'll go to sleep at a godly hour tonight like normal people. It's something to look forward to.

He strains his ear trying to listen, but he can't tell who is talking to Eva.

It overtook him suddenly: one day he was ready to fall in love, and there was Eva. She had always been there, and until then he hadn't given her another thought. Until her visits became infrequent after his father and her mother died and the war broke out, and all of a sudden he

47

started missing her. She would show up with friends, important people with money and power. She was also changing. Laughing and smoking and dressing provocatively, all things he hated in a woman. And he was dazzled.

It's not something he likes to think about. A good thing he met Salma. She was a beauty then. Her face is still beautiful, although her body rivals his in heftiness. Something soft and squishy about hers, though, as if her extra weight was not the result of overeating but of some wet tumor swelling within her.

Of the four of them (he's not counting Marie, who was born here), Salma's the one who's gotten used to being here the least. Keeps yearning for what was. His own memories are different. He can't understand why people insist on embellishing the past. It's dishonest.

His feelings for Eva written all over his face. Staying up at night thinking about her. He was green as grass back then. She took notice and started flirting. No other name for it. Her face lighting up when he entered the room, asking for his advice, making him feel wise beyond his years. And after all that, she turned him down. Cold as stone underneath her fake solicitude. Acted like it was the biggest shock of her life. They met for lunch the day after his confession, his stomach queasy with the realization he'd made a fool of himself. (God knows he'd had good practice at being the fool. His father would not be contradicted. Coexistence. Secularism. Socialism. Privately, George rejected the great man's words, sat silently while others fawned. The war came and proved him right. People closed ranks. Like with like. Maronite with Maronite, Muslim with Muslim. The days of peaceful coexistence had been an interlude stretching between flares of enduring hostility. Their cruelty was unimaginable. But his father was dead by then, and anyway, George wasn't sure the man would have conceded an inch.)

She told him she had been seeing someone. She would have considered him otherwise, truthfully she would have, although she had reservations about dating her cousin, her own flesh and blood. He didn't like her pity one bit, and it didn't help matters when she produced the object of her love the next day, a clever and slick would-be lawyer, handsome as a god.

The whole thing lasted only a few weeks, although it felt like an eternity. Now it's merely an embarrassing episode of youth.

He goes to the bedroom. Is this mana'eesh he smells in the kitchen? His stomach growls with anticipation.

He will not scold his daughter for blasting her music when she thought he couldn't hear it over the shower. Today, of all days, they must remain civilized. Today they will be soft-spoken, and perhaps at lunch they will enjoy a good conversation. And with this promise, he pats himself dry with the towel and puts on a clean shirt.

No sooner am I sitting at the table between my mother and my aunt, the one stringing beans and giving me angry looks and the other sipping her coffee and slouching in her chair, that I regret my decision to come down to the kitchen and get my mother off my back.

"Look who's finally decided to do us the honor," my mother said when I shuffled in, as if she had been calling me all this time for the satisfaction of hearing her own cleverness. I rolled my eyes, poured myself a cup of coffee, and flopped in a chair. My aunt gave me a tired look that said, "Welcome to the party."

When my mother stands up to get more beans, my aunt winks at me. "Here, you can help," my mother says, pushing the bowl across the table. I fish out a handful of beans. The string curls prettily when it comes off the pod. We work silently. My mother is considerably faster than my aunt or me, who take our time. The kitchen is cold and my mother is still giving me those half-angry looks. When I was a child, I would wash the grape leaves and smooth them out on the cutting board assembly-line fashion for my mother to put a scoop of rice and meat in the middle and roll them up like cigars. Although I would have preferred to be outside shooting baskets, it wasn't the kitchen work I minded as much as my mother using it as an excuse to pry and gripe about everything she thought was wrong with my friends and me, the neighborhood, the country.

I yawn and tuck my feet under me and rest my chin on my knees. This is all very lovely, women of three generations in the kitchen, but the only reason I am here is the female sitting next to me, drinking coffee and looking gaunt in her awful pajamas. When my mother stands at the counter to

chop an onion I look at my aunt and puff on an imaginary cigarette, joining my hands in prayer. My aunt frowns in disapproval but slips me two
cigarettes under the table I sneak under my sleeve.

Soon the air is filled with the smell of onion and garlic cooking in
olive oil. My mother washes the beans and pours them in the pan. When
she offers breakfast, I prudently reply that I will serve myself. This is what
she would have said anyway. "You'll have to fix it yourself. I'm not the
maid, last time I checked." When I was little I asked her about the meaning of *maid*, and, when she told me, I declared her half-maid and half-boss,
for which I got a couple of sharp slaps in the face. I was outraged. My
mother served and cleaned and cooked *and* bossed us around. Even at six,
I saw nuances my mother did not suspect.

I drum my fingers on the table. My aunt pours herself another coffee. When my father walks in, we straighten up and look cheerful to
avoid his sermonizing. When he wakes up in the afternoon, he scouts
the rooms looking for his lost tribe. He extends his arms and sweeps us
together to hear him pontificate. A family in harmony prospers. Look on
the bright side. His repertoire of proverbs is long. He sprinkles them in
like a good pinch of seasoning. He's learned them in English, and I suspect he's got a book hidden somewhere he looks up between customers.
Most of his sayings are pronouncements on a family's course to happiness, but he's got different ones in his stash, an assortment of good old
maxims to qualify and sanctify every possible situation and point us all
on the right path. His favorite: Rome was not built in a day. For all his
talk of harmony, he's got a temper. Still, most of the time he's nice, and
I find it sweet how he's always trying to please. Often, I like him better
than I like my mother.

"You're not eating?" he asks in English.

In my family, my father is the one constantly fretting about my eating.

"I will in a minute, dad," I say sweetly. Food is something else he
won't stop talking about once you get him going.

My aunt wants to know when he's planning to call Eva. His answer is
vague. He doesn't seem thrilled with his cousin's visit. I must investigate.

I scoop out a bit of labneh with a piece of bread and follow it with a
black olive. Pretty soon I have pulled a plate from the cupboard and am
helping myself to the labneh, cucumber, olives, and a man'oosheh.

We eat heartily, with the exception of my aunt who doesn't touch her food. My father comments on the weather between bites and proceeds to go through the list of food at the store that will have to be thrown out. The list and his calculations are long. I try to think of a proverb about gracefully accepting one's losses, but in the next minute he is declaring his intention to drive to the store.

Olives tumble to the floor. "Don't even think of it," my mother says, bending to scoop up the mess. Her tone is final. My father settles back, satisfied, it seems, as if he has detected in my mother's tone under the weary impatience a hint of the solicitude he was really seeking. I wonder if my parents still have sex.

I get a coffee at the counter and glimpse my grandmother sitting in the living room.

"Why is Teta sitting alone?" I ask.

My aunt replies that she is waiting for Eva to call.

"She can just as well wait here," my mother grumbles.

Neither my aunt nor my father answers. I consider joining my grandmother, but I must endure at least another ten minutes of this before my mother will consider me sufficiently punished for being late. It is 11:20. The next ten minutes promise to be very long. I will succumb to a massive attack of boredom. I will die right here, my face in labneh.

I let my mind take me to pleasanter things. Kevin in North Carolina. That's what normal people do on school break: go away to visit friends and relatives. Normal people *have* friends and relatives. I bite into the man'oosheh. The spices coat my palate. I pass my tongue over my oily lips and gather every last bit of zaatar.

To be honest, I miss Shirley more than I miss Kevin.

Shirley refused to let me quote Emily Dickinson in my personal statement to Berkeley. "Why always call on someone to validate your passions?" "Validate" is one of Shirley's favorite words lately. I dropped Dickinson. I gave it my all. I prepared for the SATs and got a respectable score. I revised my personal statement so many times I know it by heart. I recite it in my head.

When I was six I helped my aunt plant lilac bushes. This was my first introduction to gardening. I was thrilled with all the preliminary preparations, the visit to the nursery, the clearing away of the brush and the delivery of the loam and mulch. When my hands finally touched the dirt, I could barely contain my excitement.

Colossal lie. The little I remember from that day has more to do with all the popsicles I downed because everyone was too busy to keep track. But the dirt was a pleasure to hold when I got to it between popsicles. I remember putting a handful in my mouth and quickly spitting it out. It felt a lot better than it tasted.

Like all children, I liked searching the ground for small things: bugs, marbles, dust balls. (Even though dust balls were rare in my mother's surgically clean house. But once in a while you could find a spider web in a forgotten corner.) *In that handful of dirt I saw a whole new world: worms, small rocks, which I quickly figured out could be used as a cutting tool, and the roots of dug-out weeds that felt cool and damp on my hands and promised something creepy and illicit.*

What I loved was that everyone seemed to find it acceptable for me to play in dirt. Everyone except my mother, who carried me kicking and screaming inside the house and plunked me in the bathtub and temporarily put a stop to my vocation.

Years later, in high school, I took a gardening class after school. I couldn't wait for Wednesday afternoons for our weekly class in the local nursery. Our teacher taught us the botanical names and habitats of lilies and delphiniums, to this day two of my favorite flowers. I have kept my notes from that class to this day.

The teacher, young and inexperienced, stuttered painfully, and the students made cruel jokes, but I did enjoy the class.

Since then, I have taken charge of the backyard. It took me a while to discover my style. I use local stone to outline and add interest to a planting area. The mica sparkles in the morning light and deepens to pools of dark grays and purples at dusk.

There is a lot that I need to learn. I am interested in Berkeley because of your fine reputation and because in California, under a different sky, I believe I will learn new things. I think that a serious gardener must learn to grow plants in different climates.

I have included before and after pictures of my garden. My grandmother hopes to see me grow a fig tree in the backyard. Perhaps one day I will build a greenhouse and plant the tree.

Thank you for reading this. I hope to hear from you soon.

Sincerely,
Marie Zaydan

In California you'll have your fig tree, I say silently to Teta.

I tell my mother I'll be back soon, promise, to help with lunch but there's something I really need to do in my bedroom. She gives me a skeptical look but lets me go.

I grab my coat and boots from the closet and sneak out the back door. No one in my family is able to leave, take off alone in the world. But I don't have to worry about getting lost. My boundaries are far and wide. I have worked so hard all these years on leaving my family, I am already half gone.

THE RING JOLTS HER BACK TO THE PRESENT. Standing up from a sitting position is an effort now, both hands propping her up, her knees straightening slowly as she pauses, not quite upright, to get her bearings. Josephine beats her to the phone before she's halfway across the room.

Emilie can tell her daughter is straining to sound cheerful. Easy, child, she tells her silently. Then, before she knows it, she is the one with the receiver to her ear.

Eva sounds happy. She has never seen so much snow before and has a mind to go outside. Emilie tells her to hurry up and get here. They'll build a snowman. A fat one like Mr. Abu-Khayr, the janitor in Emilie's building. Every Saturday at ten o'clock on the dot, he would stand guard at the bottom of their building to forbid anyone from stepping on the floors he had just finished mopping. Offenders were ordered back into their apartments. Only when all six floors were thoroughly dry was the permission to come out granted with quick buzzes on the intercom, at which they quickly came out of their apartments, tearing down the stairs like children finally let out for recess.

"My frisky aunt."

"The cold is a good preservative."

"It is so beautiful here, Khalti. From my window I can see the tall buildings. It is all so clean and spacious."

"I will see you soon, inshallah," Emilie ends. She puts the receiver back in its cradle. She looks outside the window. She likes the snow, the silence and slowness its casts over the land. In her mountains, they joked how they were hibernating with the bears, their holes sweet with the roasted food. Snow is an old story of hers, interrupted when she married and moved to Beirut and resumed here, in a small New England town. She examines the neighbor's progress. The mound looks like a dome, a bubble of white shoring up the creamy house. With all her heart, she wishes him luck.

Later, she will bring him food.

LOOKING FOR PRIVACY, Josephine went to the living room to answer the phone, but she had forgotten about her mother who was still sitting on the couch. With her mother there, Josephine spoke quickly, feeling that she was being kept from saying something important. She talked about the weather, which Eva declared simply lovely, her tone anything but cheerful. Josephine remembered that tone well, her cousin suddenly snappy and Josephine teetering between anger and wretchedness. And here she was again, sweet-talking Eva into a better mood. This time Eva responded and said she couldn't wait to see them. Josephine handed the phone to her mother and walked away. In the kitchen, Salma was strategically conducting her breakfast preparations by the sink, where she was able to get a good view through the French doors.

And now she is back in her room. Josephine imagines her cousin pacing the floor, pausing to take a drag on the cigarette she has nearly forgotten in the ashtray. Casually glancing toward the window, she is seized by the beauty. So lovely, she thinks and, in the next minute, shudders. She doesn't like the snow. Her husband was killed at a winter resort. She had stayed in their chalet while he skied down the hill to the store to buy champagne, and he had died taking off his skis next to a car full of explosives. That night they would have celebrated their second anniversary. In a long letter she wrote Josephine a few months after his death, she described the twisted metal, the blood soaking the snow, her deep hatred for her country.

And yet you took sides, Josephine remembers thinking while reading the letter, fluctuating between pity and old resentments. Before you fell in love with a party man, before you could even blame it on butterflies in your stomach and weak knees, you found the war just. "What do you think, my sweet innocent cousin? With Muslims in power you and I will be wearing the veil and you'll need Georgi's permission to piss." Yet Josephine knows that her anger has little to do with Eva's politics.

Her father's bowl of beach stones sat on the coffee table in their living room. Through the clear glass, the colorful stones made a dazzling display. Josephine saw them as they once must have been, drifting before falling in a heap on the beach to be reclaimed by the water. Her father said it was that going back and forth, that incessant movement that made them fit so well into the small bowl, as if a life of movement had taught them about flexibility and the importance of stillness. They stuck their hands in the bowl and scooped out handfuls of stones and let them fall in other containers, in her mother's plastic bowls and teacups and pans, marveling at each new demonstration of spontaneous, elastic beauty. Eva was there with them, making the most noise, taking great pains to show Josephine's father how well she understood. And it was for Eva's sake, Josephine noted with a pang of jealousy, that her father had these demonstrations, in her presence that he was the most loquacious and inspired, as if his family, his usual audience, could no longer bring him to such heights. He really believed that Eva learned something from these sessions and that her heart felt the compassion for their country he tried to instill in them, the differences that in a lesser people would have been disastrous. (The war would start a few years later. How very grateful Josephine was that he hadn't lived to see it.)

Josephine didn't know what Eva got out of these sessions besides the thrill of impressing her father. Yet she must have been sensitive to the beauty of the stones. Eva caressed them thoughtfully, as if only through touch could she confirm his words. But she seemed to find her own truth in these explorations, her fingers moving slowly inside her cupped hand. Of course, Josephine imitated her. But all she got out of the experience was what she had expected, the stones in her palm nothing but themselves. Her imagination was incapable of making the leap to what her father insisted on twisting into a metaphor for the untidy heap that was their country, his belief in the possibility of peaceful coexistence. "Relax," she wanted to tell him. "We're on your side. You don't need to sway us with beach stones."

After the war broke out, Eva started working for the Christian militia. For Josephine, this meant one thing: Eva had turned her back on her father's teachings. What else, besides her father, did Josephine have to keep her cousin from pulling away?

Eva began to circulate in a new world of party people. In that world, men pulled you closely on the dance floor and blew cigar smoke over your head. Josephine sometimes went to these parties, but she usually hung back while at the same time wishing for a man to order Chartreuses and smoked salmon for her in perfect French and hating the tangle of contradictions she was becoming. It took her years to understand that with her new friends, Eva had one over on her, that she was making her pay for all the years she had had to beg for a place in Josephine's world.

It seems now so long ago when Josephine had declared in their living room in Beirut that she would never leave. Her mother pinned flowery fabric around her waist, trying to sew a skirt out of the shapeless heap cascading to the floor. During the war, clothes had become expensive, and it took all her mother's genius to keep them well clad.

"Mary, Mother of God!" she can still hear her mother exclaiming. Although a nonbeliever, her mother invoked divinity liberally, a habit she had acquired in her youth to get her sister's goat. "We might get somewhere if you didn't fidget so!"

But Josephine was pondering important questions. From the window, she could see the sun dappling the trellis. She could smell the gardenia and the tomatoes stewing in the oven. She would have to do without all this in America. At the same time, other thoughts pushed inside her head: how they lived behind a barricade of sandbags, the power failures, the lack of water, the rubble, the dust that never went away.

They arrived in America in August. Who would have expected the heat? They slumped and dragged, wondering if they'd ended up in some tropical country instead.

Once the temperature dropped, she set about reseeding the lawn. Never did she imagine that snow would be covering everything in less than three months. But when winter came, she still found reason to be pleased. In Beirut, winters were rainy, the water clogging the streets. The sky stayed gray until the first days of May, when good weather came suddenly and stayed a long time. To this day, the quietness of early storms reminds her of Sundays in Beirut, when people slept in late and the world felt hers alone. She was intensely happy then, her senses sharpened, as if the silence had removed a film that had hidden the world from her.

The snow turned the houses of Scarabee into the stuff of postcards. It reminded her of the strange excitement she had felt at the beginning of the war huddling in corridors with the neighbors. Normal life, with all its demands, had come to a halt. At first it was like being on vacation. The militias were not heavily armed yet, and the rockets fell intermittently and gave them some respite between blasts. Children stayed home from school. Women sat on the stairs with their dresses hiked up, reading coffee grounds and blithely shirking housework and husbands. Men who, before the war, had rushed to work every morning mumbling vague greetings, fumbling with attachés and coats and worrying about heart attacks in their forties, now convened for games of backgammon and cards. The snow creates for her the same feeling, a temporary sanctuary from daily life, a quiet devastation where freedom might suddenly surprise them.

Josephine immediately liked Scarabee, with its bountiful nature and tidy streets. In Beirut, they had been surrounded by cement, although they had a garden in the back, their prize for picking a first-floor apartment. In Scarabee, they owned a large plot of land that she and Marie planted with trees and flowers while her mother took care of the vegetable garden. She didn't complain about being stuck indoors for days or having to bundle up just to fetch the paper. The harshness of winter seemed fitting. She had come to a different world, and she didn't begrudge it its rhythms and seasons. She learned to like the subtle smell of the woods and the smart-looking houses behind their sturdy fences.

Yet two winters would elapse before she learned to dress for the weather. There was a bit of old world fatalism, a capitulation in the way she stumbled out trembling in freezing weather with her trench coat and bare hands, as if self-protection eluded her. Warm clothes would have been a betrayal. She wasn't ready to fully say yes to her new life. With memories of the sea still eddying in her mind, she watched like an outsider the world around her drowning in snow. It took her two years before she realized that there was no turning back and drove to Filene's Basement where she bought scarves, mittens, and a down coat.

When she had learned enough English, she went out looking for a job. She was a fast typist, but without references no one would hire her. She remembered walking into the store that now employs Marie and being turned down politely, then coming home to face Salma's rattling.

Salma had been throwing her sidelong glances that let her know five's a crowd. How much longer was she supposed to house under her roof her husband's sister and his mother? Looks that used to send Josephine to bed as soon as the sun set, and once there twitch and toss like the devil was in her. Her sister-in-law heavy with child and her brother without a job, and she and her mother two extra mouths to feed.

She turned to watching television, her ears perked to take in every word. Talk shows, soap operas, the news, old movies, she used everything. Americans are a talkative people, tidying up the world with words. If you asked her, words created their own mess. Her father treated language like a scientific experiment, carefully measuring his ingredients. She can still see him, lifting his head from the book he was reading, his black-rimmed glasses solidly planted on the tip of his nose to address her with deliberateness: if you want to know about last week's protest, you should consider reading this book. (To her and George's delight, the protest had kept them home from school, and they had watched with a great deal of fidgeting the angry mob marching on the street below their apartment. In the background, her parents talked about the rich getting richer and Israel invading, but by then Josephine's attention had shifted to more interesting things.) Of course, at ten years of age, she had no intention of reading thick volumes of history, but she learned the lesson: words had the power to explain mayhem, even when they couldn't stop it.

It snowed so often that first year that no sooner had the roads been plowed than they disappeared again under fresh layers of snow. The newly seeded lawn lay covered for months, and when spring came and the ground thawed, the tulips and daffodils sprang overnight. She was dazzled. The melting brought a wonderful surprise: a thick lawn now shimmered in the pale spring light. In the strong spines of young grass, America smiled at her. In that rescued lawn, she saw the evidence that they had come upon a land of rejuvenation, of resolute self-perfection.

Those first few years were about disguising unsightliness: hiding the concrete foundation behind boxwood, walling out the conservation land with azaleas. She would spend entire afternoons outside wielding a can of pesticide and watching the weeds die on contact. Even death seemed unremarkable here. She jumped wholeheartedly into the rational course of it, the earnest belief that certain incidents were unfortunate but necessary and one simply got on with things.

And now it is here, her American dream: a white wooden house with a large yard, and a place of business in the center of Scarabee, a small brick building with clean windows and neatly trimmed evergreens. Nothing distinguishes them from other convenience stores. It has taken a lot of work to look so inconspicuous.

Down the hill, in warm weather, cows graze in the meadows. She sees them on her way back from the store, oblivious to the world beyond their patch of grass. Sometimes, on her way back from the store, she stops the car on the side of the road and watches them. Their patient chewing sends something violent knocking in her ribs. A calf skipping over to suckle calms her. Stupid cows, she thinks as she drives away, the feeling gnawing in her that she is leaving them behind to a horrid fate. The car rounds the bend by Loom's house and begins to ascend the slope that leads to their house. Her foot eases off the gas pedal. She thinks of stopping and getting out of the car. She rehearses the things she might say to Loom, but the most she does is give a quick wave in his direction, which he seldom returns. She jerks the shift back into gear. The car grinds away on the driveway they've yet to pave, sending the gravel ricocheting. She walks in the house where her sister-in-law rattles her pots and pans. In her room, she peels off her clothes, finally free of the day. In an old dress, cigarette in hand, she stands at the window and watches Loom. She is there through the seasons: when the forsythias are in bloom and the cornstalks are tall and broad-leafed and the grass ripples down the hill, when the hayfields are golden and sway in the breeze and the trees have reddened, and, later, when the earth sparkles with snow and the trees are whipped back and forth by the wind.

Perhaps she is trying to find an answer to things. Something tells her Loom might teach her about the ways of this land. At best, Loom distracts her. (Be all that you can be, the television blared in those early days when she sat down to learn English, and she did believe it, yet didn't learn English any faster for it.)

The shock of it then when she stumbled into him at the hardware store as he was coming out of an aisle and she was readying to enter it, her head tilted to read the sign for a closet organizer she had driven to the store to purchase in a sudden urge for orderliness, intent on tidying up the mess once and for all. The cart just about hit him in the stomach, and his eyes, two blue dots, looked past her. The eyes were all she saw at first, although later she would remember his dark, clean-shaven skin and his height, about the same as hers, and the sharp creases on his twill pants, a meticulousness that mysteriously touched her. She mumbled a quick apology and ran out of the hardware store, driving around in circles in a kind of ecstasy before finding herself in front of their store where George was chatting with senior citizens. Quickly shifting into reverse, she drove home before her brother could see her.

Once in a while, a good memory turns up to fill her with yearning. Beauty alone is what she wants to remember. And in the next minute, she is embellishing her memory, summoning the green hills in her mother's town and the sheep grazing under a low sun and goats leaping off the burnished rocks. Or the Mediterranean, with its turquoise blue and the waves foaming at the rocks. She wants to select her memories like fruit at the market, plump and firm and without blemishes.

Time has done a lot to dull the edges of her resentments to something she can live with. She likes to sift through the memories and keep only the happy ones. She and Eva walking arm in arm. Tossing a ball at the beach. Eva defending her against the stuck-up girls at the school. She and Eva. The rest she tries to discard. Most of the time, she succeeds.

13

HE SMOOTHES THE SIDES one more time. When he is finished building the igloo, he will carve out an entrance and then start painting it. And the design. He wants something dazzling but has no clear ideas yet. He isn't worried. Something will come to him. He's learned this from Myra, the way she threw herself into a project, trusting knife and chisel to bring to life what was in her mind no more than the first flicker of a thought.

"Hang on to it," she'd said before casting him a rope, and he had climbed the mountain, a big stupid grin on his face when he reached the top.

"My Myra, my Myra, my Myra," he'd repeated while hugging her, reeling from the excitement, a respectable 2,800 feet of rocky terrain below them. He'd never believed he would reach the top, but there he was, panting and red-cheeked from the climb, delirious with pride.

"Why didn't you say something?" she had responded when, after being hounded for days about going mountain climbing, he'd confessed sheepishly that he was afraid of heights. "Wouldn't it be sexy," she'd wheedled, "the two of us climbing to the top then making love with the deer watching and the squirrels hoarding and the moonlight falling on your beautiful buttocks?"—these were pre-Brendan days. She waited for him to go to sleep before looking for the rope she had bought to keep their dog Husky tethered in the yard but discarded because it was too thick and, besides, she wanted Husky to roam free.

The next morning, the tent was sitting by the door. Next to it, a backpack filled with food for two days and the rope, which she looped around his waist and pulled with all her strength to put his mind at ease. In the face of such resolve, he'd had no choice but to submit.

At the top, they made love tenderly and for a long time, but she did not get to admire his buttocks. The night was cold and they stayed in their tent until hunger sent them out scurrying for kindling. He made a fire and they ate and kissed between bites. The light of the moon made her look like an angel, pale and numinous, shielding him over and over. His gratitude was immense.

The next day they made love after breakfast, this time in the open air, and a deer did stop for a few seconds to watch, which made them burst out laughing. They sat a long time admiring the view, Myra nestled between his legs, her back resting against his stomach. Casually stroking his knee, she reminded him of the first time he had asked her to marry him and she had refused. Hadn't she been the fool, she said, turning to look at him, not to know how happy he would make her? His heart skipped a beat but he pulled her back against him and closed his eyes against the recollection. Still, the day had slightly slipped away from him. On the way back, he pretended to be concentrating on keeping his balance and laughed tepidly at the jokes she told about the sight they made, tethered together by a rope. He remained silent all the way to the car. If she noticed his silence, she didn't let on. After he closed the trunk, she kissed him tenderly and loosened the knot in his chest.

His stomach grumbles again. He walks slowly toward the house, a little alarmed at the regret he feels for having a lunch of hot dogs and baked beans from a can and not something more sumptuous.

The beans slide into the pan in a wiggly lump. David stirs them with a wooden spoon, then throws in the pieces of hot dog. He eats straight from the pan, standing at the stove, dipping pieces of white bread and scooping out what he can, buttressing with a spoon when the bread threatens to disintegrate. He hates mushy bread, one of his last fastidiousnesses. When he's finished, he washes out the pan and dries it with a paper towel.

He will start carving out an entrance today. Tomorrow, he will finish the interior, and perhaps chisel scallops around the entryway. He takes out paper and markers and begins to experiment with designs. It will be a beautiful igloo, his best creation yet. It, too, will disappear eventually, and when this happens, he will find something else to build or fix.

EVA IS FULL OF HOPE when she hangs up. They might be able to start again where they left off that scorching August day, saying goodbye in the lobby of Beirut International Airport. There were tears and promises to write and visit they would not always keep. Yet despite her sadness, she was relieved to see the last of her family leave. (Her father had died in his sleep earlier that year, leaving her fully orphaned but not devastated.) A happy young wife she was that day, her arm linked to that of her gifted husband, a big apartment with expensive furnishings and the glamorous life of a political wife on her mind, and those who reminded her of the place she came from boarding the plane that would take them to the other side of the world. That part of her life excised. Yet her eyes filled with tears as she pressed her face against the large window and watched the plane disappear.

Some things never change. And so her life hasn't come as far as that. Her aunt still sharp, and Josephine still conciliatory. Still trying hard to get beyond an injury Eva doesn't remember inflicting. What Eva remembers is always being outside, waiting to be let in. And yet luck her lot, too, for being the niece and therefore part of the family, the door always wide open for her in the end. Childhood the sweetest of times. Her uncle Farid bouncing her and Josephine on his lap, the girls teasing the corners of his mustache and watching him tip his head back, push out his lips, and wag his finger at them in mock anger to make them laugh and laugh. She knows she will be welcome. Blood thicker than water. She's missed them something awful. Such great optimism she feels. Her sins forgiven. She will be taken back into the fold if she asks.

In the bathroom, she turns on the shower. The water comes down in a mist. In the land of plenty, a water-saving shower head! She feels deeply, cruelly deprived. This smattering on her body a torment, when she wants a deluge.

Her uncle's speeches swept over her like a flood. She heard him clearly, how could she help it? A practiced orator, he spoke with authority and passion, his words so vivid they played out like movies before their nodding heads. He steered them to ask what craziness has us trapped, still, in the archaic system of handing out government posts by confessional affiliation? How is this rigid system supposed to keep up with shifts in demographics? Suppose the Greek Orthodox began procreating at rates unseen? Suppose an epidemic killed off the Maronites, and the Sunnis were left to wander the earth? What then?

Then there were the Palestinians, always his beloved Palestinians, *cause du jour* of every self-respecting left-wing intellectual in Lebanon. Their slums, their diaspora. Sometimes she'd sigh impatiently. What was she supposed to do about all this? Then she'd close her eyes to shut out the treacherous voice that whispered in her ear about the boring, boring way she had been choosing to spend her afternoons lately and would open them again to see his beautiful hands striking the air in concert with his words. Much was asked of them. She would see to it that she did her part.

Her uncle and her mother died within months of each other. Eva doesn't remember grief. She remembers instead leaping straight to the state after grief, throwing herself in a stream of activities that carried her away, impatient to resume her life, her skin tingling with a mild itch. Then the war started and she joined the Christian militia, trying hard to ignore what her uncle would have said, happy for the excuse to leave the house where her father stayed confined since the death of his wife, unable to get to work when the fighting stopped, unwilling during breaks. And then happy to be gone for good when she started sleeping at the district's central office, an apartment in a run-down building with stray cats in the courtyard and bad plumbing. A mattress, a closet, and a shower were all she needed. She was cutting loose, taking her time in choosing the props of her new life.

She wasn't exactly sure why she had joined. The jumble of ideas that had once made up the core of her political convictions collapsed with her uncle's death. She believed the Christians had to be protected but wasn't sure how. She found the war loathsome but necessary. Yet she could be swayed, her beliefs easily wobbling when challenged. Around Josephine, she faked a certainty she did not feel, partly as a lark, to rouse her cousin whose wounded silence made Eva mean. Yet she would have done anything for a little peace and quiet when her aunt started pestering her about leaving the apartment and the party. "Won't you come to your senses, habibti?" It was crazy, pure madness, she said, Christian pitted against Muslim. Only George came to her defense. To him, the war was unavoidable. But Eva paid him no attention. He was the wearisome little cousin who talked too much and hid the radio away in his room so that he might storm in and deliver the latest news with such an air of urgent and bumptious agitation, it made her want to laugh and knock off his head simultaneously.

In the months that followed, she thought about following her aunt's advice and finding a new place to live. The militia men who greeted her politely when they came to the apartment were the same ones who pranced in the streets, armed to the teeth. They were feared and revered, but, most of all, they were loved. Everyone had a son, a brother, or a nephew in the party. And so, when they made the most of their power, when they cut in front of a long line at a gas station or fired their Kalashnikovs in the air to disperse the crowd, they were quickly forgiven. Anyone who complained was frostily reminded of the incredible toll the war took on the men's nerves.

She liked some of them, the young ones, barely out of high school, eager to defend the cause and preserve the share of power negotiated in 1943. After dinner they helped her with the dishes and told her about the girls they were dating and those they planned to woo. It had automatically fallen on her, like an immutable law of nature, to tidy up and cook. She did not mind. She was living there rent-free, waiting for something she could afford to come along, and making enough money in the meantime from the office work she did for the party to get by. When she was in a bad mood, they took over the cooking and shrugged off mocking jeers about doing women's work.

There were always people coming and going. Sometimes an important figure, the party's lawyer or a unit leader, would appear, and the men would shut themselves in a room and talk for hours. A few women, girl-friends and sisters, sometimes visited, bringing clean clothes and cigarettes. Eva felt grateful for the company. They took up the two couches in the living room to talk about fashion and crack dirty jokes. They rarely mentioned the war and left within an hour of their arrival, chattering nonstop on their way down, their arms full of dirty laundry. At dinner-time, alone with the men, Eva would listen to stories about their battles, her ears ringing with the violence of their tales, and imagine her uncle sitting in the corner, his brows knotted in disapproval.

For a while she had a crush on a man named Elie for the sole reason that he disapproved of crude language. The others were intimidated by him, and when he came, they were on their best behavior. From a wealthy section of Achrafieh, an eastern suburb, he was the only son of a civil engineer and a doctor, and heir to a restaurant business his grandfather had started in the Forties. He treated her with great consideration, refilling her glass and standing when she left the table to tend to the dinner. Elie could have gone to study in France. He was in the engineering program at the Université Saint-Joseph, where classes had been halted indefinitely. Instead he stayed, lecturing without affectation, sharing generously from his expensive wine reserve, fighting in battles often enough to mollify any class resentments.

They fought for this: to preserve the power structure that had protected the Christian minority by allowing them a slightly favored status in the government. They saw themselves as more modern than the Muslims, more open to the West, better educated, even though many of the fighters came from the mountains, from small villages that had seen little modernity.

Even when the streets were quiet, the violence lingered like a foul smell, threatening to erupt any minute. The nights were particularly difficult. This is when the fighters would return to the apartment, leaving their weapons in a heap by the door instead of in the first floor apartment where the munitions were stored, and move about silently like cats, unable to sleep, standing vigil over the shadows. She would sit in the kitchen with a glass of water and glance at them. Their eyes were red from the drugs they took when they thought she was too busy to notice.

She was surprised by this thoughtfulness to which they still clung, and it was what allowed her to stay instead of running out into the night.

It was worse when some of them didn't come back, and she went to their funerals and watched their mothers and sisters beat their chests and wail.

But then what choice did they have? The Muslim Lebanese were out to destroy them, and so were the Palestinians, and, if one believed the rumors, men from all the over the Muslim world, from Somalia and Sudan and Yemen and the rest of the Middle East, had joined the fight. A picture of the enemy flickered hazily in her mind. She had never met a Muslim.

What she saw on that summer day while on vacation at her mother's and aunt's house in the mountains did not qualify as an encounter. Some said he was a Somali, others a Yemeni, and others still that he had come all the way from Bangladesh. He'd been captured in battle, with the crescent moon dangling from a chain around his neck and hatred flaring from his eyes.

She and Josephine had been plucking walnuts from the tree and breaking them open with a stone. Neither of them could have guessed the violence brewing in the square. As they gathered the empty shells, they heard the commotion and looked up. A boy running with his friends stopped to tell them about the head of a Muslim on a stick. They looked at him as though he was insane, but the noise in the square was getting louder. Josephine struck her stone at the tree and walked back to the house while Eva and the boy ran toward the noise.

In the square, a man standing on a platform jabbed the air with a pole on which a head was impaled. With each of his jabs, a cry rose from the crowd. Shielding her face from the sun, Eva saw a bald scalp and eyelids so swollen they seemed to have taken over the entire face. In the crowd, she recognized the owner of the hostel, Sitt Houda, whose green thumb had created a prodigious garden. The faces of other people she knew flashed before her: the one-eyed grocer who sat on his stool all day while his wife tended to the customers and Maryam who could catch a chicken, wring its neck, pluck and gut it, and hand it to you in a sack before you had finished pondering the fresh eggs. Eva looked back at the head, now huge against the blue sky. It teetered on the pole but didn't seem in danger of falling, as if buoyed up by the crowd's excitement. The rank odor of sweat permeated the air and made her nauseous. Slowly she walked back to the house, stopping at the water fountain to wash her hands stained by the green skin of the walnuts.

Her aunt refused to stay another day, but Eva's father would not interrupt his vacation for what he considered the fleeting folly of a people on edge. Eva spent the last days of the summer in the house that was now too big and empty without Josephine to talk to about the head that came to torment her at night. In the days that followed, life in the town returned to normal. People went on their daily promenades, the church bells tolled for the ten o'clock mass, and the kaa'k vendors woke her every morning with their calls. Eva waited for summer to be over so she, too, could leave and put it behind her.

When she started living at the apartment, memories of that summer came back. She was afraid to wake up one morning and find the spoils of a battle on the coffee table. Yet she did not go out of her way to find a new place to live. It was easier to stay put and watch her bundle of money grow while the men came and went around her. Then one night she was ambushed by a newcomer, a man named Samir with too much arak in his blood. She was never in any danger. As soon as he had grabbed her by the waist and asked drunkenly to see what was under her blouse, the others had wrestled him the sofa where he passed out. But after that she saw herself as she must have appeared to him, someone who must have been there for one reason alone, so that they might do with her as they wished. The next day she found a small room in a convent run by the Sisters of Nazareth. It was clean and cheap. She moved her meager possessions and, for the first time in months, slept peacefully and without dreams.

Because she needed the money, she kept her job. Once in a while she would go to their parties. There were always interesting people to meet, men who tried to seduce her and with whom she flirted but always let down at the end of the night. She made sure to place herself in the vicinity of men she would enjoy meeting, men who spent money without ostentation, who were courteous and well read. She steered clear of the flashy ones, the parvenus who had arrived by their ruthlessness, to whom fell the shadowy activities, the torture and the killings, and who came back the next night drenched in gold and expensive perfume to partake of the celebrations with the party's elite. They got their pick of the ladies because they were loaded and spent generously, but they retained the tightfisted, calculating astuteness of their earlier, humbler lives. They were unimportant. She was acutely aware of the class system that allowed very few men of modest means and no women to rise through the ranks. Eva was getting tired of trying to find a justification for the war. The men remained a mystery, in turn pious and cruel, gluing pictures of the Virgin Mary on their Kalashnikovs and shooting women and children at close range, yet finding the time between battles to fix the houses of their aging parents.

Around this time she met Robert. When she was introduced to her future husband, she liked him instantly. He was tall and bearded and he called her Eve. "Eve, the mother of womanhood," he said with a big smile. It was a corny line but he seemed pleased with himself. Her heart thudded in her chest. A few months later they were married.

Robert's mind was as neat and logical as a mathematical theorem. She never saw him pray or enter a church, and he didn't seem to have any strong opinions about God, yet he called himself a Christian. It was simply an immutable part of who he was, a mental gene that identified him as fully as the DNA that gave him his dark hair and his height. Never was one so coolly rational and at the same time so traditional. While the separatists exaggerated Lebanon's Phoenician origins to the exclusion of any other, he saw no contradiction in being a Christian Arab. He was not afraid of recognizing the brew of Persians and Turks, Aramaeans and Greeks, and especially the Arabs of the peninsula that had intermingled on their shores. The enemy was not a lesser people but an adversary who had to be fought and coaxed into sharing power. War was a means to an end. He would as soon not fight. His words relieved the doubts of the last several months. Here was a man who, like her uncle, pursued reason and distrusted excess, was both practical and virtuous. She sank wholly in him. The enemy turned into a partner in a business transaction fraught with high-stakes dealings yet contested as coolly and shrewdly as a game of chess. The violence seemed almost rational now that he had revealed its purpose.

Had he lived, he would have become an important figure in the party and in a unity government after the war. The bomb that exploded while he was taking off his skis had been intended to kill random civilians. It wounded seven, all of whom would survive. He alone was killed, dying on the spot. When she learned of his death, she threw up again and again, even when her body had nothing more to expel. Even when she could barely lift her head off the pillow, she still heaved.

She turns her back to the shower in the futile hope the weak jet might relax her aching shoulders. She quit the party after Robert's death. Rival Christian militias waged bloody wars on each other. The Muslims had proved as cruel and reckless. She was done with politics.

So she wandered in her apartment with Marietta and her cats. She threw parties, shopped for Beluga caviar and French cheese, and taught Marietta how to make pepper-crusted tuna. At her dinner parties, they listened to classical music, switching to Arabic music at the end of the night. The women wound scarves around their hips and belly danced while keeping a close eye on their husbands. Undeserved or not, Eva had a reputation for snaring men. She always released them promptly, however.

Eva taking what's not hers. Her life incompletely launched and so she helps herself to the possessions of others. Breaking her mother's prized rosary one day, a present flown all the way from St. Fátima in Portugal especially for her, the saintly woman who spent her days and the better part of her nights praying. The blue beads glinting on the tile floor. Eva felt bad for her mother and went down on her hands and knees to help look for the beads. On impulse she swallowed one, and, but for the pity that held her back, she would have swallowed them all to see them disappear and discover what it would be like to have a real mother who made a home for her. She hated herself for going back over and over again to her uncle and aunt's first-floor apartment, seeking asylum, nuzzling against them like a lost animal. A mother who did not prattle on about God and the church, good and evil and everlasting life, but was more like her aunt with her feet sturdily planted in the here and now, pinching dead blossoms and painting the balcony railing a deep ocher, and listening to Um Kulthum on the porch glider sing her prodigiously long melodies while a few thin clouds floated through the starry sky. A rosary in her stomach was the prize Eva was willing to pay for having such a mother. Yet it didn't make a difference at all. Her mother substituted her own knuckle for the missing bead.

She steps out of the shower and ties a towel around her chest. Her feet sink in the plush carpet as she makes her way to the bed. The room is rank with cigarette smoke. She opens the window and lets the icy wind in, then shuts it quickly and climbs into bed. There, wrapped in a white towel and a rough hotel blanket and shivering with the cold, she imagines their reunion as she sees herself walking into their house and putting down luggage, back at long last. And with this thought, she closes her eyes and sleeps a brief and fitful sleep.

IF HE HAD HIS WAY, he'd have a mountain smooth as glass. Emilie sees him from where she is sitting facing the sliding door, nothing but the gray sky and snow dunes around him, so faint now he seems like a dream she has made up.

Smooth slippery glass to keep out the intruders.

Of course, you don't know that for sure, she hears Shirin saying. The way you don't know for sure that God doesn't exist.

After Farid died, Shirin stomped in, peremptory and unflinching.

"People see the light right before they die," she announced. An urgent need to make things right overtakes them, to turn heavenward and repent. Farid was no exception.

"Oh, but I do know and don't ask me why or how, just accept it," Emilie fired back in the face of this new resolve.

This was a pitiful explanation, but she couldn't bear her own flesh and blood planting uncertainties in her way. She couldn't understand why Shirin insisted on telling lies about her husband: how, sensing his own death, he had turned into a believer, how, once again, he had failed to tell her his innermost thoughts.

Shirin's hair was tied back as tightly as ever, stretching her eyes and lips upward. Once in a while her eyes would open wide, determined to resist the tyranny of that hair.

"I know what I know," was Shirin's only answer.

Until that day, Shirin had tagged along docilely, an unquestioning audience to Emilie's rebellions. At the age of ten, mass had become so tedious that Emilie would sooner deny the existence of God than set foot in another church. No one listened and no one answered her prayers. Her words were lost in the hollow silence. Such waste, she thought, feeling humiliated by this divine indifference.

Prayer defined Shirin wholly, squeezed out other possibilities that might have developed, given half a chance. In exchange for her sister's compliance, Emilie looked the other way, pretending not to mind when Shirin interrupted their visits to leave the room and pray. Her prayer schedule was as regulated as the sun rising and setting, and nothing might interfere with it.

When Eva started coming regularly, Emilie took her in. The child had been abandoned. They did not talk about her mother's obsession with prayer, but it lurked in the shadows of Eva's neediness and Emilie's giving. What did her sister want so much that she spent long hours on her knees begging for it? That everything else, motherhood, sisterhood, life in general, had to wait while the beast was fed?

That face: carnivorous. Emilie was repulsed. She had liked her sister better before, when she stumbled behind chimeras, sweetly vulnerable in her hunger.

Emilie faltered. What insight did her sister's words harbor? What did she know? Had Shirin guessed how much Emilie had given in to her daughter?

Farid was their pretext. Emilie asked her sister to stop spreading rumors about her husband's alleged conversion, but Shirin would not relent. They did not speak for several weeks. Of course later, when Shirin lay wasting with cancer, Emilie was right there wiping her brow and anything else that needed wiping and pretending she believed her; Yes, Shirin, yes, whatever you say, yes, my dearest.

If he had his way, her neighbor's mound would have no ripples or bumps, she argues with the ghost of her sister. Snow as hard as stone and a glassy surface no living person could climb. But he doesn't have his way. Can't possibly build a mountain and fuss about its looks too, so the bumps and ripples can't be helped. She is afraid for him, afraid that he might take this snow falling as a sign that he must be entombed.

The heaters sputter. Water gurgles in the pipes. Mold spreads on the walls. In the kitchen, George clears his throat. Her daughter-in-law moves from the sink to the stove and back. Josephine and Marie have disappeared again and are dreaming of a different life. Everywhere in the house she detects the ghosts of sounds, the snoring and the shuffling, the chewing and sighing, the hushed-up rebukes, the small rebellions, the accumulated sounds of living.

Here, she has learned, noise is a sign of low breeding. Life moves quietly like a soft, rubber ball rolling across the floor.

She looks longingly at the bony curve of the telephone. Already she wants to talk to Eva again. She doesn't know her niece's hotel number and she doesn't want to ask Josephine for it. She can barely read and write. For the first time, she realizes all the things she misses, even the rudimentary knowledge of her furtive schooling.

But food she knows. In the garden she grows tomatoes and peppers, herbs and beans, cucumbers and squash, and three varieties of lettuce. She knows that okra must be fried golden brown first so that it won't turn slimy in the cooking. And secrets: a drawer full of carved statues, a wooden egg in her pocket, a neighbor raising a mountain around his loneliness.

16

SPRAWLED ON THE GROUND and making snow angels, I close my eyes against the blowing snow. Above me, a blanket of swirling white. A hulking figure I must seem, seen from up high, stuffed in winter clothing. I lick the snow off my lips. Sandwiched between a good layer of it and, deep beneath me, the damp sleeping earth, whose sluggish pulse I can almost feel. Whose sleep I don't mind, even though I can barely wait for spring to get my hands on the tightly closed bulbs and the young shoots of grass.

Who wouldn't be tempted to surrender to the ice and wind? I will be here when the earth returns. Not in Scarabee, but still waiting, on the lookout for the earth to wake up.

Yes, I will wait in California. Studying to be a horticulturist, as I was always meant to be. Even before my grandmother gave me the withered fig and told me that planting a fig tree was like planting a miracle. Before I knew fig trees didn't survive in the north without a great deal of pampering and covering up in the cold months with burlap, which must have meant one thing: the cold climate was deeply resistant to miracles; and so I slept at first with the seeds under my pillow, waiting for the day when I would have the skill to sow wonders and create what nature herself was loath to give of her own free will. My grandmother in the meantime teaching me Arabic songs, and me, a child still, guessing at the yearning in the melody, flinching a little with its sorrow at the same time I molded my voice and words to my grandmother's. Feeling in my own heart a mysterious tie with a past I preferred represented only by my grandmother, who was so much more tolerant than my parents and, when she talked, a great deal more fun to be around.

Meant for horticulture before I pulled the can of poison from my aunt's hand and told her she was doing a horrid thing, killing those poor, innocent plants for the sole reason she didn't like the way they looked. I convinced my aunt to put down her poisons and simply pull the offending weeds. I know my aunt keeps a bottle of weed killer hidden in the garage, just in case.

Berkeley is not my choice because a fig tree can grow there unhindered, saturated with sun and mild breeze, but because it's as far as I can get from Scarabee. I imagine myself on campus, walking into a world ruled by gardeners, strolling down gravel roads, clippers at the ready, snipping off scraggly shoots, invigorating where I find listlessness, evermore the beautifier.

I went as far as to have it carved on my body, a clover the size of a quarter above my navel. A declaration of love. My parents will scream murder. I will stare at them coldly, a bag slung over my shoulder, my hand upon the doorknob.

Clover sprawls in clusters over the lawn, sending my aunt a little over the edge. I am appalled that weeds must be punished for their vigor. I wonder how I will tackle them as a master gardener. I let them mix with the grass but pull them out from among the flowers and the vegetables, where they can take over. I see the problem of weeds as a great moral dilemma.

For now the earth is covered with snow. People who like snow see variations. The way it cleaves to the trees, how far down the branches bend, the angle of their submission. And here and there, icicles like so many jewels, a gaudy spectacle.

I loved the snow when I was a child. With Shirley I made demented-looking snowmen and had snowball wars. And even then, I felt the urge to turn my back on the creaking heaters and the hot cocoa waiting in my mother's sanitized house, and break away without a second look. With my aunt Josephine, I took turns jumping from the top porch stair and landing with a thud, the snow growing more compact with each leap. We promised to try out the neighboring airport for parachuting lessons, but we never made good on our promise. My aunt said she was not afraid of flying as long as she knew the landing would be safe. I secretly pitied her lack of ambition.

I shut my eyes and send ESP to the admissions officer at Berkeley. Marie Zaydan. A gardener. I will change my name. Myrian. Muriel. Zadi, Zade, Muriel Zade.

My mind takes me to practical matters. When I walk, I am always conscious of treading on a dance of life and death. I try to imagine what the garden will look like in the spring and remember how I left things in the fall. When I am on my knees weeding, digging, transplanting, my mind races ahead to a life totally devoted to gardening. No homesick mother or controlling father, no love-struck aunt or mute grandmother. Perhaps that's what I thought the first time I dug my hands in dirt and exorcised my family. Something solid buttressed me. After that, transforming the backyard into a blossoming garden was like a new birth.

I sit up. The wind dies down for a few seconds and Loom's mound flashes. To my right is our house: a white colonial with red shutters, built in the late 1800s. My mother would have preferred a new house. Who can blame her? Why be saddled with the ghosts of strangers when it's all she can do to keep her own past under control? Because of its color, the house seems to be one with the snow. I am a stranger looking in, imagining the lives within. This is the kitchen where the family gathers for meals. This is where the man and the woman of the house lie, and the young lady with her trinkets and anger, and the sister, a spinster who doesn't know yet that she has a crush on the neighbor, and the old woman who hasn't talked very much in the last few years but who taught her granddaughter to hold on to a dream. Their lives can be summed up this way. I feel kinder toward my folks. Right here and right now, their quarrels seem small and unimportant.

It's getting cold, but I don't want to go back in yet. There is my house, and there is Loom's to the north and Shirley's to the west. A solid triangle. My unbearable compass.

H E C I R C L E S W H A T H E H A S, taking stock. He lifts his eyes to the top
of the mound, and it is like offering his face to sharp needles. The snow
is falling aslant now. He drives the blade deep into the heap lying at his
feet. What he scoops up to hurl at the mound is wet and heavy, clinging
where it falls.

"David, David," he hears her saying. Voices from the past are his only
companions.

"When will you give me a grandchild?" his mother said in her thick
New York accent. Myra laughed when he told her his mother had been
leaving messages on his voice mail at work, exhorting him to fulfill his
duty and multiply. Mother Nail File, as they called her because of her grat-
ing voice, was often the butt of their jokes. Guiltily, he said he wished
sometimes they would lay off a little, stop before his mother was sacrificed at the altar of their glee. His wife opened her eyes wide in surprise
and said, "But Dave, you know I love your mother!"

She called him Dave when mildly objecting to something he had said,
without anger. And it was true about her loving his mother. Myra invited
her over for dinner at least once a week (they called her Mother Froufrou
when they were better disposed, for all the lace she wore) and was better
than he was at calling her and reminding her to take her medications.
Although his mother had lost her formidableness, and was now an older
and lonely woman, he still avoided her, as if her power might reawaken
on contact and leap out at him. But for all her good will, Myra refused to
talk about children. His mother knew that of the two of them, he was the
easier to hound.

Myra's pregnancy came as a complete surprise. Throughout their marriage, she had hinted at the possibility of remaining childless, the two of them together enough to keep them going for the rest of their lives. He wasn't sure how he felt about having no children. He did not consider them essential to his happiness, yet a part of him hoped he would be a father. He was careful to hide his happiness at the news, but she saw through him and hurled objects at the wall. Nothing he said or did alleviated her mood. She calmed down in the second trimester, fascinated by the fluttering that grew bolder every day in her swollen belly. She began to joke again about David's mother who had, she said, resorted to witchery to foil the science that had kept Myra bare all these years despite frequent and responsive sex. Relieved, he joined in on these jokes. They pretended to sniff at the goodies that Madam Enchantress, as they called her now that she was believed to possess magical powers, concocted for the health and vigor of her daughter-in-law and her long-awaited grandchild.

Myra's pregnancy proved difficult. She had to give up her job at the dance studio where she taught ballet to young girls, and David's mother spent a lot of time at their place. Mother, as she was now simply called, exhorted the younger woman to rest, made her ginger tea to aid her digestion, propped her feet up on pillows, and spent the rest of her time cleaning the house and knitting little outfits. Myra was amused but confessed that the attentions made her a little weary. Still, she let herself be pampered and thoroughly settled into her life of inactivity.

Labor was long and difficult. David and Myra were grateful when his mother stayed to take care of Brendan. They were humbled by her efficiency. When one of them still attempted a joke at her expense, the way, for example, she gave Brendan her pinkie and imitated his sucking motions or how, an inveterate Catholic, she took him promptly to the Polish church for a pre-baptismal blessing should calamity strike and bar his entrance to heaven, the other would laugh tepidly and change the subject. They felt indebted and helpless, and barely objected when she started spiriting him away to church every Sunday, even though the two of them were, if not complete atheists, at least dogged skeptics.

Although David did not raise any objections, having convinced himself of the temporary nature of their arrangement, his old resentments resurfaced. He remembered being dragged to church every week to sit in utter boredom, his mind wandering spitefully to matters blasphemous. His father would occasionally come to his rescue and keep him home despite his wife's protests. Unfortunately, he often slept in on the weekends, well into the late morning hours and long after David's mother had already grabbed him by the hand and dragged him outside to stride in the freezing air to St. Patrick's where the hoodlums lay slumped against the wall snoring loudly and terrifying him. David's father died when he was eleven, and the boy lost his only, albeit ineffectual, ally.

David worried that Myra was all too readily relinquishing the care of their son to his mother. Yet he kept quiet, reminding himself how difficult the pregnancy and labor had been. When, six months after Brendan's birth, his mother died of a massive stroke, Myra and David were devastated. Myra blamed herself for burdening the older woman. David, on the other hand, could barely forgive himself for his thinly disguised brusqueness, from which he protected his son and wife by spending as much time as possible in the office.

For a while they were marked by guilt. Myra, after participating from a distance in rearing their child when his mother was alive, gave up her job at the dance studio to devote herself completely to Brendan. She read books on child rearing, nursed Brendan well into his third year, and banned television. As for David, he became a bastion of even-temperedness and collected every photo he possessed of his parents to inculcate in the child a sense of family. Yet their guilt-induced virtuousness eventually exhausted its course, and soon they were themselves again. Occasionally, Myra lost patience with Brendan and left him with David who distracted him with junk food and the fiendish TV. One day, David put away his parents' pictures and never brought them out again.

They were right in ridding themselves of guilt. Never did anyone any good. Useless emotion, if there ever was one. And yet, it came and went in its own time. One day the sins of the world were on your shoulders, and the next you were marvelously delivered. The world kept going with or without you, with its aches and triumphs, its cruel indifference. He likes the latter feeling, but he is well conversed with guilt's course to know that he is not there yet. He throws himself back into shoveling. Expiation or numbing physical labor, he knows he must stand here in the tumbling snow for a long time still before grace rains upon him.

IT ISN'T AS IF she hasn't pondered this before and turned it over in her brain so often and so carefully, it has taken shape and emerged before her like a frieze she unfurls and pauses to point at this or that scene. This is where it all started, she would say. And this, right here, is where I wouldn't allow it to go on.

It isn't as if this is the first time Emilie has tried to loosen the gnarls of her past. But today she does it with a new urgency. The sky brooding and heavy, and Eva coming, and the necessity she feels of pulling up her sleeves and getting on with it, wherever it might lead her.

Right from the start, she was on to him. In her memory, their first night wasn't lovely and amorous but an initiation into suspicion. What she remembers is her husband revealing his plans for them to move to Beirut while she is sitting on the bed, straight as a board, wondering how he might deceive her next.

Farid didn't tell her about Yussef right away, as though she wouldn't notice his coming home late every Tuesday and Thursday. It immediately raised the alarm in her head, even before she decided to investigate and found out that, with the exception of a few nuns and the cleaning staff, no one lingered after hours at the school on those days, least of all her own husband. But it was only after Josephine was born that she decided to speak up. Money had been disappearing for years, but now every lira lost meant another opportunity missed for her baby daughter. One night she waited up. They would have it out, come what may.

But she would have to wait until the next day. That was all he would say that night. A teacher through and through, he believed in showing before telling. He was stalling. She shut her eyes and thought of throwing something heavy at his head.

She braced herself for the worst. Another woman? She didn't believe this for a second yet couldn't come up with something more original.

Sleep was long in coming that night. Shortly before daybreak, she finally managed to doze off for what felt like seconds before his hand on her shoulder startled her awake. She stumbled half-asleep into the kitchen to prepare the coffee and got dressed while he ate a quick breakfast of labneh and olives.

They walked together into the pale morning light, Josephine clasped to her bosom, their destination, it turned out, a neighborhood she crossed regularly on her weekly visits to the butcher's. A noisy place, with shoe shiners and fresh juice bars at every corner, and narrow, congested streets. They entered a gray building with laundry hanging on the lines and a cluster of dirty children in the courtyard. The elevator smelled of urine and hiccupped its way to the third floor where they got out.

Farid knocked three times on one of the doors then produced a key, which he used to let them in. She took one step following her husband, then another into a small hallway that led to a badly lit room. A tall man was standing in the living room, dressed in an undershirt and pajama pants and surrounded by litter: a pile of newspaper on the only sofa, full ashtrays, thick dust on the floor, grime on the only window. The man was in as sorry a state as his apartment. He obviously needed a bath, and when he opened his mouth to give them what might have been a broad smile but could have just as well been a grimace, Emilie saw that he was missing several teeth.

"This is my brother, Yussef," her husband said, looking at her from the corner of his eye, pausing to allow the words to sink in. Emilie looked at him without understanding, searching her brain for clues to what exactly he might have meant by "brother."

"My wife, Emilie," he added without bothering to look at Yussef (the tall man, as she called him in her head). If he said anything else, she doesn't remember. Her mind was in a thick fog. She vaguely recalls him clicking his heels like a toy soldier (did she invent this silly detail to get back at him, to make him look ridiculous and out of place?) before making a dash for the kitchen where she scrambled after him, her arms, still holding Josephine, the only part of her body with conscious feeling.

The sink was full of dirty dishes. Calmly, Farid rolled up his sleeves and began washing them. She was speechless. At home he never lifted a finger.

"Explain," she demanded, simply.

He shut the water off, looked around for a towel and, not finding one, leaned over and rested his wrists over the sink. His sleeves were soaking wet, his rump was stuck up in the air, and he had soap in his hair from when he had smoothed it back earlier. Under different circumstances, she would have laughed.

"He got sick when he was eighteen," he began, still avoiding her eyes. "I knew he had been taking drugs. I could hear my parents talking at night. Sometimes he slept for days without a peep. Other nights he'd stay up ranting about creatures that made a racket and kept him awake.

"The doctor wanted him institutionalized. When they heard this, my parents were furious. He was on drugs. That was what was wrong with him. They sent him to live with the monks in the mountains, hoping they would cure him.

"He was gone almost a year. It was the best time I'd had since his illness. I didn't have to lie in bed wondering if this was going to be one of those nights no one got any sleep, or rack my brain to come up with clever answers to offer the neighbors who hoped they might learn more from a young boy than they did from his tight-lipped parents. The official line was that he was not well, and we never wavered from it.

"We could tell right away when he came back that he was not much improved. He no longer brought up the creatures. We didn't know if they had left him for good, since now he no longer talked. It was as though without his imaginary companions, he no longer had any reason to communicate with the outside world. In a way, he seemed worse than before, lonelier. Still, from where I stood, things looked far better. I didn't realize until much later, after my mother's death, when I became the sole caretaker of my brother, how much she had had to do for him because he could not attend to himself. But at the time I was simply happy that he wasn't so visibly out of it anymore."

Emilie shifted her weight to one foot. The words were now tumbling out of him, and Farid didn't seem to want to leave anything out. He was still leaning over the sink and looking intently at the drain as if into a well from which he pulled his memories. She sat down. Josephine yawned and smacked her lips, as if savoring the memory of some tasty meal. Emilie patted her head soothingly.

"I promised my parents that I would always look out for him. Not a day would go by without one of them reminding me of that promise. When my father died, my mother became even more tireless, as if she were now on double duty. She was terrified that I might lock him up in a mental hospital after she was gone. It was always Yussef this and Yussef that.

"When she died I only wanted to get away from him. That's when I went to live in the village. I told myself it was only for a short while, until I could take care of him full time. I had lived in the shadow of his illness since I was a child, and I needed to be away for a while. I visited him often, sometimes every day. I was feeling all that guilt. I kept imagining all the ways he might hurt himself. It was out of the question for me to take him to the village. All my life, my parents had hidden his condition from the outside world. In the city, people were less likely to notice a poor, crazy fellow who barely opened his mouth. Then, when I met you, I became even more guarded. Your parents might have rejected me if they had found out about him.

"You can see now why I wouldn't tell you my plans before we married. If you refused, I would have had to leave without you."

He looked quickly at the door then put a hand on her shoulder and leaned over. "I am ashamed of him." He gave her a sad smile, adding, "Now you know the kind of man you have married."

Emilie was too angry to feel sorry for him. Once again he had concealed things from her. Ordinarily, she saw herself as someone with sound judgment and a good mind despite her lack of schooling. But every once in a while, she was reminded that her husband might have seen gaps in her education so unbridgeable they made it impossible for him to unburden his heart, and jealousy and doubt reared their ugly heads.

Yet he looked so sad that her heart began to soften. "You should have told me," she said.

She wanted to be alone to take stock of the situation. Her husband had once again deceived her and she had a crazy brother-in-law. (Only the doctors called it an illness then, a term she herself would adopt, but much later.) He would never be cured. They, she and Farid, would have to take care of him for the rest of their lives. They would never commit him to one of those awful hospitals. She wasn't sure how many there were in the city, no more than a handful probably. She had seen one of them once, a concrete building you came to after rounding a sharp bend, half of it hidden behind a high concrete wall.

In the living room, Yussef was sitting on a pile of newspapers. She walked to the window and looked out. She could see the courtyard below where the children were kicking a ball. Framed by the tops of neighboring buildings, a small square of sky looked bloated with impending rain. A strip of weak light fell through the dirty window on the dusty upholstery.

She found a relatively clean chair and sat in it, erect, careful not to lean back against the stained cloth. Her eyes gazed around the room, stopping to examine the black-and-white family picture on the wall. She had never known her parents-in-law, who died before she met Farid. She could not tell from the picture what kind of family they had been. It was a formal picture, with everyone looking up from the corner of their eyes at the ceiling, something she had noticed in other old photographs that people did back in those days, either to avoid looking at the flash or to give an illusion of naturalness, as if the camera had caught them unawares, and always, mysteriously, looking up at a point above them. Yussef was a head taller than Farid. Emilie saw in the photo a close resemblance between the brothers, although she would have been hard pressed to find it now.

Josephine wrinkled her face and yawned. It was customary then to keep infants wrapped tightly in a blanket to prevent bow legs, so that all one was able to see, emerging from what looked like a giant chrysalis, was a little hairy knob, red with frustration at having its body so swaddled. Josephine started to bawl but just as quickly quieted down and fell back asleep, probably finding the effort of trying to wiggle as much as her little toe too great for the time being.

Emilie had hoped to busy herself with the baby and have an excuse to stay silent. A quick glance at her watch revealed they'd been in the apartment a whole hour. She was beginning to wonder whether she shouldn't be heading back home without Farid when he came out and asked while buttoning his sleeves whether his brother needed anything.

"Cigarettes and soda," Yussef said. She was startled to hear him talk, as if she expected him to communicate by signals. She got ready to stand, but Farid motioned her to stay. He pretended not to notice the furious look she gave him and left (ran off was more like it, she thought, leaving her to her fate) with the promise he would return quickly.

She tried to sort out the implications. Of course she would not stop Farid from taking care of his brother. Yet she wished she had not demanded to know the truth. Foolishly, she had not allowed her husband to keep on protecting her. Yussef wasn't someone one introduced to friends or invited over. He was needy as a child. He was filthy. Her stomach heaved just looking at his undershirt. She wasn't sure what would be expected of her now. Nothing, she hoped. Farid had done a good enough job on his own so far. At the same time, she didn't like her thoughts one bit. She felt a twinge of guilt and smiled weakly at Yussef.

She could barely contain her relief when her husband returned with orange soda and two cartons of cigarettes. Straightening a few pillows and dusting the coffee table, as if a light tidying up was everything the place needed, her husband instructed his brother to eat the green beans in the refrigerator. With this, he looked at her and they left the apartment.

On the street she took several deep breaths, insisting on carrying Josephine the whole way back to their apartment and giving Farid reproachful looks when he offered to relieve her.

A week went by, and Yussef didn't leave her mind. Despite her intentions to let Farid continue to handle things alone, soon she was visiting Yussef regularly. At first she brought him food and sat only a short while, trying awkwardly to make conversation. Yet her eyes were always wandering off to settle on some revolting area, barely believing the degree of filth they saw. One day she showed up with a bucket full of detergents and cleaning tools and got to work. She declared war, focusing on a single room every day until, by the end of the week, the apartment had turned into a respectable, if still somewhat shabby, residence, with glinting floors and polished furniture. Next, she held out a garbage bag and commanded Yussef to dispose of his crusty undershirt and all irredeemable clothing. His wardrobe was considerably diminished as a result, so she checked the tags for his measurements and bought him replacements. A hamper started filling up with dirty laundry on a regular basis, and she decided that the progress he was making was well worth the work she was putting into his restoration.

He always acted with utmost politeness, greeting her when she arrived and thanking her before she left, yet he still didn't talk in between. He would sit listening to the radio or reading the newspaper while she went about her chores, breaking the silence occasionally to ask him whether he preferred stew or roasted lamb for the next visit.

Sometimes she would look at him from the corner of her eye, wondering when she was going to see a display of his craziness. If these displays ever occurred, she missed them entirely. Sure, he was not what one would call social, and every once in a while he would stare at her blankly as if she had come from another planet. But if these were indications of madness, then half the world needed to be locked up!

One day she set the table for two, and from that day on it became their habit to eat lunch together. The conversation flagged, but she could talk for two. She had the distinct impression he listened carefully to her words. Every once in a while, he would nod vigorously at something she had said. When she noticed that he kept rereading his old newspapers, she started buying him new ones from the grocer around the corner. He would read while she worked, and when he was finished he would toss the new paper in the old pile, which, despite her complaints, he refused to throw out.

Once in a while, Emilie felt impatient with all the filth he could produce. He still bathed infrequently, and Farid didn't press him to wash more often or offer to help him do it. In fact, her husband seemed to have absolved himself of responsibility toward his brother and was happy to let her be in charge.

Soon, fall had come to an end, and it was followed by a rainy winter that kept Emilie home more often than she would have liked, wondering how Yussef was getting on. When spring arrived, Emilie's spirit brightened, although the air turned warm and heavy, already carrying in it a prelude of the summer heat. Emilie worried when she thought ahead to the summer, when they would have to part with Yussef to vacation in the village.

Up until that time, Josephine had slept peacefully while her mother cleaned and cooked and her uncle read his paper. Emilie was amazed at how much her daughter could sleep, and had even consulted a doctor who had given the baby a clean bill of health and told Emilie to thank her lucky

stars. Pretty soon, Emilie was wondering if she had jinxed her good fortune. Almost overnight, from a placid baby Josephine turned into a lively
toddler always on the go, a despot in piggy tails who whined and clam-
ored for attention. Josephine was too old now for the mummy swathe.
Unbound, she was fixed on making up for lost time.

Yussef proved to be a gifted guardian. The discovery pleased Emilie
to no end. She would watch him with her daughter, proud like a mother
who was witnessing at last the blossoming of a timid child. A gentle,
patient child who indulged with good nature his younger partner's bud-
ding urge for power. Who would pick up, again and again, the same toy
Josephine insisted on dropping, and keep coming up with new games
to see each one greeted with shrieks of rejection. Emily could do her
work in peace knowing that Yussef was in charge, and for this she was
profoundly grateful.

Farid, who until then had been happy to see her take over the responsibility of his brother, began to complain that she was spending too much
time at the apartment, exposing Josephine to a part of their lives he wanted
to keep secret. Emilie was shocked to realize that, for all her husband's
talks of tolerance, the mentally ill (as she had started calling Yussef, madness to her being a state of raving lunacy, fire and spittle) had not earned
the price of admittance into his just society. She wouldn't hear of limiting
her visits. Yussef had come a long way, and her husband was simply jealous of her part in his improvement.

She had it all wrong, he bellowed one day. Yussef almost choked a
man to his death once. He'd promised himself never to tell a soul, but
since she persisted in exposing their only child to unnamable risks, he
had to speak.

He pulled her down next him on the couch, but she moved away to
the other side, meaning for the distance between them to stop his words
from reaching her and unraveling her patient work.

"To this day I don't know what really happened," he began, signify-
ing with a wave of his hands that only a higher power might elucidate
the mystery of his brother. Yussef had never before acted violently. ("Nor
has he since then, but that's beside the point. He is not well, Emilie. You
can't tell what he'll do next.") She blocked her ears, yet a few words made
their way to her brain. Something about being at the beach and Farid

disappearing for a few minutes to buy kazoz and returning to find Yussef choking a stranger.

"The point is, Emilie," he said, "it happened once, and I don't want you or Josephine there when it happens again."

She edged further away, trying to look unflappable.

In the days that followed, she thought about Farid's words more than she let on. In a short time, she had come to know too much. Since the revelation of Yussef's existence, she had begun to doubt if she, an uneducated villager, would be any more welcomed than Yussef in her husband's tolerant society. And now this: gentle Yussef had tried once to kill a man for no apparent reason.

One by one, memories of odd behaviors would return to disturb her sleep. Memories she had suppressed, wrapped up as she was in the progress he was making and that she supervised with the zeal and dogged optimism of a reformer. She remembered him once squatting, his head between his knees, rocking on the balls of his feet and making plaintive sounds like a wounded dog. And when she closed her eyes, she could hear the sighs he made, sighs so frequent they blended with his natural breathing. And various other oddities that made the hair on her skin stand on end ever so slightly, enough to turn on the little red light in her brain. But when she returned the next day, he was always the same gentle man who played with Josephine with the patience of a saint. She tried to ignore Farid's warnings, but, as she would shortly find out, this proved unsuccessful.

The day was particularly beautiful, a sunny April morning with a lovely blue sky and a mild breeze that ruffled the orange blossoms. It had rained the night before and the sun glinted off the wet leaves.

There were the usual skirmishes along the border with Israel. Emilie noticed that Yussef seemed interested in the news, and she tried to keep Josephine quiet when he listened to the radio. To Emilie, the south seemed like a world away.

When she arrived that morning, Yussef was listening to the radio. She set the table and chattered on about their favorite topic, Josephine's latest milestones. The day before, she had taken five steps, and Emilie was busily recounting how Josephine had lurched forward then dropped on her buffered behind and clapped. Ordinarily, Yussef would respond with a smile or make a sound that told Emilie he was listening. But today he was silent. Emilie didn't mind and went on talking, then left him in charge of Josephine to get lunch started.

It was his smell she noticed first. It overpowered the smell from the tomato stew she was stirring in the pot and the garlic mash she had made for the roasted chicken. She felt him getting closer until she knew he was standing right behind her. Her mind worked fast. She uttered his name, expecting him to back away, but instead he put his hand on her shoulder. It was the lightest touch, like a small insect crawling on her skin, and that she might have flicked away with her finger. She was dizzy with the heat from the stove and the air in the apartment, which was still and heavy despite the window she had opened the moment she arrived. Suddenly she felt a sharp pain in her hands. She thought he must have attacked her with something sharp, and she was panicking at the thought of what he might do to Josephine next. Then she realized that she had been holding on to the hot pot with her bare hands. She turned around to face him, and with a shock realized that he had beautiful eyes. A sound escaped her lips, a sob or a scream, that made him dart to the living room and, before she could stop him, pick up Josephine and look at her as if seeing her for the first time. She doesn't remember how she pulled her daughter out of his arms and bolted out of the apartment.

That night, Farid, who rarely showed anger, cursed and pounded the table. Emilie realized she should have kept silent. She'd had time to think about the events of that morning and recognize that she had probably overreacted. Yet she didn't try to calm her husband.

Farid started the procedures that would put his brother in a mental hospital the following day. Within a week, Yussef had disappeared from their lives. If he visited him, Farid never brought it up. Then George was born. As the years passed, sometimes Yussef's name would come up, and she and Farid would fall quiet. Emilie tried to guess if, like her, Farid wondered if the events of that April morning had been no more than the excuse they had been waiting for, that they had inflated their significance to get rid of Yussef.

Years later, after Farid had died and the war had broken out, she tried to find her brother-in-law. Beirut was now divided. A friend who was a Red Cross volunteer and moved around the city with relative safety managed to bring her the sad news. Yussef had died of a heart attack during the war. She prayed that the hospital had a bomb shelter. She could not bear the thought of Yussef standing the way she remembered him in his living room, waiting patiently to be guided.

Poor Farid with his load of secrets. She knew them, the ones that mattered, and she let him have them. Burdened. As if he was the only one with secrets. The good dancer, the thinker, the star of his school. She let him get away with things. Together they sent his brother to the madhouse. They shared this unkindness. For this she let him have his secrets and didn't reach out to him when later, for different reasons, he lay by her side consumed with remorse. For this she didn't comfort him, and she punished him every day for the rest of their lives.

She goes to the kitchen and pleads with Salma. Let me take care of lunch. Salma shrugs her shoulders. Let me, she insists. Emilie leads her daughter-in-law by the arm to the living room. The younger woman sinks, unprotesting, to the sofa. Surprised by her easy victory, Emilie returns to the kitchen. She brushes the table clean and brings out parsley and ground meat from the refrigerator and tampers with the day's menu.

19

THE TELEVISION BEAMS IMAGES from Baghdad. Lying down on the couch, Salma tries to ignore them but can't, and finally sits up to watch. The camera pans the desert dotted with charred tanks and plumes of black smoke rising in the hazy sky, then jump cuts to a young correspondent who speaks breathlessly while pointing at the rubble behind him. She tries to listen, to compare what she sees on the screen against her own recollections of war, hiding in a suburb of Beirut while the bombs exploded around her, her head between her knees as if trying to disappear within herself. But the young man's words wash over her. This war is remote, the TV screening her from any kinship she might feel with people she doesn't see. The images can disappear in a click, the war vanish in the stream of daily life. This is all she can do. This is the extent of her sympathy offering, this sitting up to watch, despite her best efforts to shut her eyes.

"Have you turned down the thermostat again?" She knows that George hasn't moved from his chair since her mother-in-law shooed her out of her own kitchen and plopped her unceremoniously on the couch, but she asks anyway for the diversion her question might bring. George ignores her.

"You have to hand it to the Americans," he says. Then, immediately, "They'll make a mess of things."

She sighs in irritation. She is never sure where he stands on the war. Yet she is grateful, for his words bring back her usual complaints, and in this thawing produced by the humdrum and vague dissatisfactions of ordinary life, she tilts back to rest once again.

She has never trusted happiness to enter her fully. She would let herself experience it stealthily, in secret, as if the absence of witnesses precluded the possibility of being required to pay a price.

"Salma ya Salama," her sisters would sing and climb the cherry tree and toss her fruit, although she could have just as easily reached it from her ladder, thank you very much. She was a big girl and didn't need their help, but they chuckled and stuck out their red tongues and tossed the fruit all the same while dangling their legs in front of her face. Her sisters the twins, you couldn't tell them apart, and that seemed to give them extra daring. Despite the hot sun she shivered, as much from climbing the ladder to show them she was as good as her word, although she was terrified of heights, as from seeing her sisters perched high in the tree, and she thought, "We might lose all of this." The week before it had rained for days and the dam could barely hold the river back, and this is when the thought first entered her mind that very little stood between them and death. She trembled at the possibility of losing her sisters forever, and losing this morning with its sun burning the last few clouds in the blue sky and their house and the stream behind it meandering down the mountain like a vein feeding the earth. She thought that, as long as there was breath in her lungs, she would have to be on her guard, for there was evil in the world.

So she froze on the ladder and the blood drained from her fingers and toes, and, holding her breath, she told herself, "As long as I don't let it out, we will be here forever. Just don't let it out, and everything will be all right." The sky shimmered. If you held still, the air itself became visible and enveloped everything like a silky film. But her sisters noticed something was up and came down from the tree, laughing like the whole thing was a game. They pried her hands away and laid her on the grass kicking and screaming and letting the precious air out of her lungs. She understood that day that all she would ever manage to save was her own skin, if she was lucky. Her sisters slapped her cheeks and jumped around her, flitting in and out of her vision, which was blinded by the sun filtering through the treetops. The two of them were unable to sit still, as if a motor was running through their legs and the switch had gotten jammed, and the only way to turn them off was to take their skinny bodies and bang them against the wall.

Salma felt the first stirring that day. A nugget of anger hot against her chest. She couldn't name its source. It was an abstract, universal anger, a sense that there was something about the world she fundamentally rejected. But after her sisters had run off to swim in the stream, she opened her arms and, cradling all she could of what was out there, the sun and the smell of grass and jasmine and the dusty stone, she pulled it all in to keep as long as it would stay, and thought how she would never get rid of this fear.

She reopens her eyes. On the screen, a flashback to the beginning of the invasion. The aircraft fly through a disembodied sky. Baghdad is plunged in darkness. Not even the massive explosions can fully illuminate it. The tanks roll through the desert. A country has been captured. Defeated Iraqi soldiers file by and squat under the cool gaze of American soldiers, hands clasped behind their heads, looking relieved to be caught. The pictures are reminders of how easily victory has been achieved, as if ordained by divine will rather than the predictable outcome of superior weaponry. Now she feels dreadful. They have done it again, gone off to kill each other, and she will watch and know that, despite her best efforts to remain untouched, her heart will break. Once again war is here, and she must sit and watch.

She didn't know the first thing about weapons, so George took her to the roof of their building and explained the difference between a Katyusha, an RPG, and an M16. Standing side by side, they watched the fighting, back then still confined to the center of the city. It was all a muddle to her, and she didn't know why he insisted on teaching her something she didn't care to learn. She pretended to listen, but when they returned to their apartment she would hurry to the kitchen, to her pots and pans, and sing.

One day a tank appeared in their neighborhood and positioned itself in front of their apartment building, taking aim at the city in the west across the dividing line. They couldn't sleep that night as they waited for the tank to start firing. They took turns watching it as it sat still and silent under the big pine tree, a huge animal crouching in the dark. The next day, it opened fire. The ground shook with every shell that went out and every one that came in retaliation.

The tank stayed there three full days, and on the second day Salma returned to her pots, singing loudly through the bombs.

People wondered what held her together. They wondered at her milky skin and the calm way she moved across a room. Night after night, she and George would rush to the underground shelter, grabbing on their way the small suitcase they kept by the door for their bare necessities. In the shelter, she would not look at her neighbors and at their crying children. She blocked her nose against the smell of their unwashed bodies, and sang in silence while sitting erect on her mat, her feet shod in good shoes. Evasion became her art. She staked her survival on it and fiercely harnessed her imagination, which would have taken her, had she let it, to the buildings gaping with holes and the craters on the roads, to the sniper who had taken over their neighborhood and riddled a line of blood and fire between them and the rest of the city, to the shattered glass and the dead bodies, to the infernal dance of the bombs on the ghost city. She held her breath as she had done once under the cherry tree. If she let down her guard, she was done for. That much she knew.

George watched her closely, unsure what to make of her calm. She didn't know why she allowed him one day to prod and push her to hurry up, to put his hand on the small of her back on their way to the shelter and raise her rhythm to his. Perhaps it was because she was young and felt guilty about all the singing she kept to herself, until she felt smooth and hard, unscarred like polished stone. But suddenly, there was his hand on her back pushing her to go faster. After that, she started cowering in corners during battles.

She waited patiently for things to return to normal. When George was out, she sang. Once he had loved her voice, had wrapped his arms around her and told her he was the luckiest man alive. Now, he accused her of frivolity, of thriving on catastrophes. He began to snap about little things: weak coffee, a rip in his socks. She knew he was frustrated, but didn't forgive him any more for it. She didn't know how things had come down to this. She had the feeling that she had lost something precious and irretrievable.

Their apartment had two balconies on opposite sides of the building. The one on the west side, the one they called the blue balcony because of the blue railing, had a view of the building across the street where the sniper had taken up residence. She kept the curtains drawn in the room adjoining the balcony. They spent most of their time there, George reading the paper and she sewing. The room was often dark because they seldom had power, and they bumped into each other and tried not to snap.

George started mentioning America. He was a glazier, and for a while business was good. People were still willing to replace their broken panels. But when the war didn't show any signs of ending, their standards plummeted, and thick plastic sheets were adequate to shelter them against the mild winters of Beirut.

Salma tried to make George change his mind about leaving, but it was like talking to a wall. He would come home early from the shop and sleep all afternoon. Eventually, he stopped going to work altogether.

So she made her bargain with God. Plant a child in my belly and I will go to America. Why a child in return for America? Perhaps she knew their leaving was inevitable and that, of anything she might have taken, a child would turn out to be the most permanent. Now she knows she was wrong in staking her survival on a child.

She should have known better than to let God in on the deal, because he took the singing out of her. The minute she made that deal her voice disappeared. Her child was her biggest temptation, the light of her life, but also the death of her voice.

In the TV studio, a general points at a map of Iraq, explaining where the enemy is still holding on, which cities have fallen. She thinks about cooking. She is a good cook, although her olfactory senses have gone through great changes. Used to be able to sniff a dish and detect its layers, her nose her instrument for precise classification, cinnamon nutmeg paprika clove red white black pepper separating, reconstituting themselves, briefly pure and whole again in the highly efficient halls of her nose. Now the flavors blend and merge and merely whisper their scents.

Earlier, before her mother-in-law had shooed her out of her own kitchen, she'd rubbed the leg of lamb with olive oil and thyme and slit the meat for garlic cloves. She'd browned the vermicelli in butter before adding the rice.

"It'll all spoil," George had said, scooping a large dollop of labneh from the bowl with a piece of bread. Pita bread, they called it. Thick and small when the real thing was large and thin, made for rolls, not pockets. Her mother would prepare the dough in the morning and roll it into thin wheels she would stack on a tray and cover with a damp towel. The two of them would walk to the bakery, her mother rushing ahead and Salma trailing behind, skipping over the cracks on the tiled sidewalk. They walked quietly into the dimly lit bakery as if they were entering a church, leaving footprints on the flour-coated floor. Salma would lean against the counter and watch the baker line up three round loaves on his pallet and slide them in the fire oven. Within seconds they would puff out like golden balloons, and the baker would bring them tumbling onto a big wooden table where they slowly deflated, fragrant and steamy in the yeasty air.

"Let it go," she had said to George, and breathed a sigh of relief when he and Josephine left the kitchen. When her mother-in-law had ushered her after the both of them, she didn't resist. Ordinarily, she refused to let anyone else do the cooking. But her mother-in-law might have been intimating her desire for a truce, and Salma didn't want to seem difficult.

"Really showed Saddam this time," George is saying. And then, invariably, a cancellation: "He's not the last or worst tyrant, so what's gotten into them?" Disgusted, he switches off the TV and starts reading yesterday's paper. Salma knows that she will get an earful if she asks about the war, so she remains silent.

Her blunder was so small. Waking up this morning with a craving for eggs and a desire to please, she had brought the terra-cotta pan from the attic. By the time the butter had melted, her mother-in-law was seated in her usual chair facing the stove and Salma was full of cheer, wiping her hands on her apron and smoothing her hair back the way her sisters used to say she did when she is trying to please. "What is up with Salma ya Salama? What fresh sins to be forgiven now?" they teased. Eva had already called, and Emilie was looking glum, which Salma blamed on the news of the delay. Not that her mother-in-law was usually chirpy, but Salma was ready to forgive worse slights in her generous disposition this morning.

She was aware of Emilie watching as she prepared the eggs. Not very fresh, but the yellow taut and round and holding together in the hot grease. The edges brown and crisp before she slid them onto a plate and broke four more in the pan. A feast of eggs was what she had in mind. Some extravagance, like chopped parsley sprinkled on top, strips of fried ham curled along the edges. For once she didn't mind the snow. She even found beauty in the gray and white, the leafless trees looking less stark with their loaded limbs. A fury of death she would learn to respect, if not exactly love. Unleashed forces that brought her close to a state of reconciliation with an alien nature she had so far mistrusted.

A few more eggs and the drizzle of parsley and ham, and she was ready to deploy her creation amidst the blue dahlias of the tablecloth and the pitchers of juice and milk (no cartons or plastic gallons today). Ready to begin serving, ladylike today, between fork and spoon, the festooned eggs with edges precise and clean like a picture in a magazine. Ready to slide a plate toward her mother-in-law, smiling, aware that she was trying too hard (but she was trying, dammit!), that some days she was capable of closing up and confounding everyone around her, and that today would not be one of those days. In the way her mother-in-law picked at her plate, Salma remembered that Emilie liked her eggs scrambled. And now Salma, who had used up all the eggs, could not undo what had been done. She took the plate and walked first to the trash bin where she threw the eggs, and next to the sink where she washed the dishes, her back to her mother-in-law. Once in a while she looked through the window and across the large expanse of what only a few weeks ago had been the lawn and a thriving vegetable garden, and which was now entirely covered with snow.

She could see their neighbor shoveling. The way he had been at it all morning, you would think snow was the work of the devil. A grave is how she saw it. Beaten back into the earth and gone for good is what it should be, if you asked her. Once in a while she glanced at the reflection of her mother-in-law in the window. Sitt Emilie, she called her in private, with a mocking lilt on the Sitt and with the air of putting her hands on her hips and seesawing her shoulders. The older woman was giving her the silent treatment. Salma bristled under the prickly stare of these eyes, and under the weight of the silence she created a slew of accusations. She didn't exactly know what charges she imagined her mother-in-law harboring. Emilie had been there all of Salma's married life, first in Beirut and here the last eighteen years. Tired of feeling scrutinized but unsure of what she had to hide, Salma, married at sixteen and now thirty-six, has had enough.

When she is really angry, Salma resorts to the French *Madame*. So, Madame Emilie was staring at a point on Salma's back, waiting for her to apologize. Eva was trapped in New York. Emilie was disappointed. All week she had been counting the days. Salma knew how longing could take up every waking hour. And then to come to this: a stupid storm and no Eva. All the same, it was no reason for Emilie to be rude just because Salma cooked her eggs wrong. If you asked her.

Especially since she, Salma, would have to do all the work. All the cleaning and the cooking would have to be redone once the roads cleared and Eva was finally on her way to Scarabee.

She rinsed the last of the eggs down the drain, washed the plate, and put it on the drain board to dry. The terra-cotta pan was a drudgery to clean. She picked at the crust with her fingers. A scouring pad would have ruined the coating. She worked vigorously, stopping once in a while to rinse her hands.

Pretty soon, the pan was clean and she dried it. People started coming in. Josephine poured herself a cup of coffee. George looked around for something to eat before his shower. Salma had a mind to tell him about their daughter lounging in her room, but the last thing she wanted this morning was a scene between these two, so she told him about Eva's call instead. After a good deal of pondering, as if everything, however insignificant, deserved careful deliberation, he decided to take a shower before checking in on his cousin. But first, he preyed on a banana. His prominent stomach pulled his pajamas up, making the front of the legs look too short. She made a mental note to buy him new ones. A far cry from the man she married, but the years haven't been kind to her either. The sum of the extra weight they have amassed between them amounts to that of a young adult. Surplus flesh pours from their middles and bars the possibility of a third presence on the sofa. Day after day they sit there, her largeness freezing her into immobility, while George fills every atom of his with relish.

She opens one eye to peer at him. Most of him is hidden behind the newspaper. His fingers are hairy sausages clutching the page.

She has to admit that she was looking forward to Eva's visit, although she's heard nothing good about the woman. Squandering her husband's money, no children to tie her down, and a new man every few months. Not the kind of influence she wants around Marie, but it has been a long time since they've had company. Once, there was a Lebanese priest who spent the night on his way to a parish in Rhode Island. He was a noisy eater and he left his used earplugs on the floor by the bed for her to pick up. She was glad when he left. Another time, a Lebanese family moved into town, but by the end of the first year they had left for California on account of the mild winters and the man's brother opening a restaurant. The man said his brother could use the help, but George would hear none of it. He was not working for any man but himself. It wreaked havoc in their household. She craved the good weather and the figs that the woman, who'd lived there briefly, kept reporting—a boastful sort, she was, always showing off and criticizing, saying how she would never raise her daughter in the middle of nowhere without a Lebanese community to impart solid values. Salma and George fought constantly during those days. After dragging her halfway around the world, he now refused to take her to a place that would remind her of home. "A dishwasher," he cried, throwing his arms in the air. "My wife wants me to be a dishwasher!" In vain she told him he'd make it to manager in no time. He kept shouting while his mother and sister listened without intervening, their silence speaking words, if you asked her. It made her love him less. And it made her distrustful. There was no one in the world she could count on after this.

When she finished washing the pan, she packed it carefully in newspaper, as she had wrapped it eighteen years earlier in her hand luggage under spare underwear and dried figs and carried it through customs and long airport stops. She was six weeks pregnant and no visible belly yet, but already nearly doubling up from the pain in her back, surviving on dried fruit and water. She put the pan near the stairs to take back to the attic once she had a few minutes.

"The pan!" she exclaims, bolting out of the living room, panicked at the thought of her careless daughter stampeding down the stairs and sending the pan crashing into a million pieces. Her precious pan with its layers of flavors and well-greased coating. But there it is, still waiting on the first step where she left it. She clutches it against her chest. The newspaper is now soft and thin, the writing faded. It seems silly, but she couldn't bear it if her pan broke.

For the third time in one morning, she climbs the stairs. Very quickly she is reminded why she doesn't do this every day. Her knees strain with the effort. She stops at the landing to catch her breath. There is no sound coming from her daughter's room. She is tempted to knock, but she makes herself walk on. Twice already today she's pounded on the door and demanded that her daughter turn down the music, but now she has no excuse.

In the attic, she finds the box where she keeps the pan tucked under the bed sheets that were part of her dowry and that she unwrapped once and quickly put away. Their fussy, old-fashioned embroidery stood out in the small, low-ceilinged guest room with the single window, mounted so high in the wall she must stand on her toes to open it.

"You gotta keep it simple here," George says. "No fuss, no muss." She doesn't know why Lebanese people insist on speaking English amongst themselves, in over their heads with American idioms. She takes the sheets out. Perhaps she'll put them on the bed in the guest room for Eva's visit.

There is a box of Marie's old toys she has been meaning to take to the Salvation Army. There's the electric piano with the missing keys. Any musical ambitions she might have entertained for Marie were quickly destroyed by her daughter's complete indifference.

"Sing, Salma, sing," her grandfather used to say. "All work and no play will kill you," he used to tell her father who was early to bed and early to rise and no play in between. Bent over paperwork he brought from the bank, her father ignored her grandfather, whose whiskey breath undermined his authority. Her mother tried to distract her husband with elaborate dishes. Salma sang for the same reason, while her sisters sewed silently. By then, joy had left them. They plodded on, thin and weary, as if they didn't know where to begin to tackle all the things they must. They sewed, their fingers sheathed in thimbles, their bony wrists tireless, already lost to her. She looked across the room at her grandfather slouched in a chair and started to sing. Instantly, his face lit up like somebody had given him a bundle of money and told him there was more where that came from, and he sat up and sucked on his water pipe and slapped his knees. The water bubbled and the smoke that came out of his mouth was warm and fragrant. He tap-tapped on his leg and swayed his head and clucked his tongue, an orchestra all by himself, and joy filled the room and put a smile on everyone's lips. There was nothing you could do about it, no stifling joy once it came out, so you might as well give yourself to the moment. That day, forgetting her caution, she abandoned herself to joy. Until her father walked in and said, "You can't hear yourself think in this noise."

The bundle of paper her father brought home kept getting bigger, until her mother found him one morning face down in June's account. According to the doctor, his heart had given out at midnight. He looked small, his gray hair, greased that morning with pomade, matted around his face. She had not pulled him into the singing, she thought with regret. Then, with less regret, she thought how he had always been busy with his work, and how they'd had to sit still and silent like monks and wait for him to be finished. It wasn't the sitting still that she minded but the silence. If her body kept time at bay by not moving, her voice, like a healthy animal, needed its daily exercise. Angry words came out of her mouth and reached her mother's ears. Salma had never seen her mother furious before. "You will not speak ill of the dead." Her mother pointed at him lying on the couch in his Sunday best, and at the living room around them and added, "See everything that he has been busy providing us all these years." But all Salma saw was her dead father lying as if he were asleep, as if he might wake up any minute and tell them to be quiet and stifle their living.

Her sisters are married now. They live near each other, in houses built by their husbands who are also brothers. She imagines them interrupting their sewing to remember their outings in the cherry orchard. Perhaps they talk about the comfortable life she must now lead in the United States. Every once in a while one of them calls. They hate giving bad news and dispense it in small doses, like bitter medicine. When they telephoned eleven years ago and mentioned their mother's health in passing, she knew enough to take the first plane home. She arrived just in time. Her mother died the next day. Salma sang to her, without spirit. She was no longer sure singing was all her grandfather had made it out to be.

She lifts one of Marie's toys to her face. It is so small she can see parts of her face at a time and the effect is unflattering. One day she was no longer beautiful. She saw it in George's eyes. She didn't know why she had changed, only that it happened here, in this country.

True, it's a beautiful land, but the beauty doesn't touch her heart. Marie and Josephine break their backs in the yard. Her daughter, the gardener, lectures. "See how the house is framed by the junipers, and how the red of the Japanese maple pulls the eye toward it so you don't notice the asymmetry of the house?" Salma doesn't have a clue what her daughter is saying, but she pretends to listen. Marie is onto her bluff, because she drops everything and leaves in a huff. Perhaps if she spoke better English, or if Marie's Arabic were less rudimentary.

Her parents' house in Lebanon, a large box of massive stone and tiled roof, sat in the center of a courtyard surrounded by pine trees and a wrought iron fence. In the front was the polished stone of the court-yard and the colorful drizzle of potted begonia and geranium her mother planted year round, and in the back, leaving almost no room between itself and the house, a stone wall supporting the high earth and a dozen or so mulberry trees. Wildflowers cascaded down the wall. Salma doesn't remember her mother fussing with the garden. What she remembers is the trust her people put in nature to take its own sensible course, and the sense that the house, and they, had been there for a long time.

So much open space you don't know what to do with it. Even their house in Scarabee seems like one large room, the walls knocked down by the previous owners to create what they call here an open floor plan, as if bringing people together is a matter for the architects. In Lebanon, a house was revealed a room at a time. There was the "salon," a formal living room where visitors were received. Seldom were they allowed into the rest of the house. Salma sits taller with the memory of such delicacy. She observes here none of these shades of modesty in human relationships, finds something deeply false about the way people are tossed together and expected to commune instantly, as if they were cut of the same cloth. The torture of sitting through parent gatherings at Marie's school, smiling uneasily as people lay their hands familiarly on her arm, and thinking how she'd not be able to eat any of the hummus she had brought because so many hands had descended upon the bowl to scoop with their chips and their vegetables.

The grayness began during their first year in Scarabee. Josephine, who was learning the language faster than any of them, told them about the homeless people and the babies left in the trash. The war seemed mild next to this. Salma started avoiding the news hour, but the grayness did not go away. It crept from the keyholes and the vents in the floor and hung in the air, until it seemed that the house had generated its own clouds, perpetually blotting the sun.

Her grandfather would be disappointed to see her today. When she looks in the mirror, she sees an old woman whose skin no longer knows how to hold on to her bones. Every night, she covers her face with cream and waits for a miracle. But none occurs, and when she washes the cream off at the sink, the same face stares back at her, and she wants to cry.

Sometimes he feels heavy as a corpse. Puttering about all day, and at nightfall collapsing like a dead weight who would as soon not wake up the next day to go through it all over again. Calamitous, the way he drifts into sleep. And yet isn't this what he prepares for all day, flooding himself with activity so he can go out like a light in an exhausted fit of sleep? The couch he sneaks glances at now from the corner of his eye beckoning for just this kind of respite. And yet he turns his back to it, feeling about in his pockets for his pack of cigarettes. He has come inside for a pee, is what he tells himself, even if it's only half the truth. He checks himself in the long mirror, as though to confirm he's still in his coat and boots and won't have to miss a minute getting ready to go back outside. The only waste is in stopping to grab a new pair of gloves from the closet, and off he goes.

Nothing wrong with standing on the porch to light up a cigarette before recommencing his digging, the flame dying a few times in his cupped hands before taking. Nothing wrong, either, with hard, tedious labor, although right about now he's thankful for the break this smoke allows. He remembers his mother sitting on the couch and folding laundry, the faraway look in her eyes belying the brisk efficiency of her fingers. Peering at her from behind the glass door, he felt he had caught her in a lie, allowing herself to be carried away from the kind of domestic tasks she made believe punctuated a life of virtue.

Myra was lax about the housework. In the end, he'd had to hire a housekeeper, with the house untended and no clean laundry for weeks. Despite his own tidy nature, he was relieved to find his wife and mother so different, although Myra's intense devotion to Brendan would cause him great anxiety eventually, fearing he might lose her to compulsive motherhood, his mother's biggest failing.

When Brendan entered kindergarten, Myra returned to sculpting, her passion before dance. She carved small wooden figurines instead of the large statues of clay and stone she had once created; economy was all she could manage in the little free time she now had. Once again she was the woman he had fallen in love with twelve years earlier, with a fury for truth and beauty. They had met during their senior year in college, and everything that wasn't her after that became a blur: the commute through the last slushy days of winter, and the long, tedious classes he couldn't wait to leave to be with her. He knew the number of moles on her skin. He could tell when she was getting her period from the way the skin under her eyes darkened to a deep purple, and her body became puffy with water.

After she and Brendan died, he packed everything that reminded him of them and put the boxes in the attic. He had too many haunting regrets to reckon with without physical reminders.

His friends checked in. At first he received them in his living room, where he sat in unlaundered pajamas saying little and waiting patiently for their departure. Soon he stopped answering the bell. He spent most of his days in bed with the curtains drawn. When he happened to look at his reflection in the mirror, a stranger stared back at him, a face with matted hair and haggard eyes and a gray, sparse beard. He lost weight and had to secure his pants with a belt. He was licking his wounds, sinking deeply in a cottony haze from which he had no intention of emerging.

He pulled out by the most fortuitous of events, finding Furlo the Frog under a chair one day, his hand roaming unconsciously after a night of bourbon that had ended with him sprawled on the rug of the living room, sonorously drunk. He had neglected to turn on the heat, and the cold had wakened him. He stared at Furlo and started to weep. When he had exhausted himself, he sat up. He rocked back and forth with his arms wrapped around his knees and decided that memories would be honored. He took a shower and shaved and cut his hair, clotting the sink with clumps of gray and brown. He did the laundry and scrubbed the floor before he called the real estate agent. Keeping his eyes closed, his finger roamed the map and landed on Vermont. A house not too big, he told the Realtor, with woods in the back. Preferably no neighbors.

A kind of rage to fix and clean overtook him. He swept the gutters, fixed the tiles on the roof, nailed in new wood on the deck. And when the weather became warm, he painted the house and brought down the boxes from the attic and left them by the door, Furlo the Frog lying on a pile of books, to be hauled on the truck that would take him to Vermont.

JOSEPHINE IS ANGRIER THAN SHE SHOULD BE. She wishes she were still in the kitchen, stringing beans or slapping seasoning onto the leg of lamb and irritating Salma. Anything to avoid calling as she promised she would. Yet here she is, rehearsing the words she will soon speak, and here is her hand reaching eagerly for the phone.

A high-pitched voice answers after the first ring. Without delay she is connected to Eva's room.

Eva sounds sleepy, as if the call has woken her.

Josephine remembers her cousin's mood swings, the way she never knew what to expect next. She listens patiently while Eva complains about the breakfast she was served at the restaurant.

"How does it look on your end?" Josephine asks.

"Like it's the damned North Pole." The novelty must have worn off since their last conversation.

When in doubt, always ask about the "situation," the Lebanese's euphemism for the war and, later, the general collapse that ensued.

"Everything's obscenely expensive, but we get by," Eva replies.

Like always. Josephine bites the words back. The feeling returns that she has escaped something vile. She looks at the immaculate fields. In one of her talkative moods, Salma said that, at heart, Josephine was really an American, with her love for independence, her wanting to be left alone. Cold and selfish is what she really meant to say.

A woman of leisure for once, she thinks, stretching on her bed, lighting another cigarette, going to the window to see what Loom has been up to since the last time she looked. "We have a neighbor. Marie has named him Loom," Josephine says. "I'll tell you all about him." She wants to talk about Loom to someone her own age.

"Time was all we had during the war," Eva says.

Obviously, Loom hasn't made an impression. Or else Eva is playing one of her games, teasing Josephine and thwarting her attempt to lure Eva back with shared secrets.

"We're getting old."

Josephine imagines her cousin propped up against the pillows, surrounded by nail varnish and makeup boxes, and smiles. She can't stand the fragrance, and Eva will do her best to keep a bare face, but will make it a point to repeat how naked she feels without her makeup, without even a trace of lipstick.

Love, still, after all these years.

And the other side of love, the unrequited, slighted part.

It was always like this with Eva: her damned confidence. Wherever did she get her boldness, her ensnaring ease, as if she knew things no one else did? In her presence, Josephine's lips unsealed, new ground was broken, thoughts she never knew she harbored sprung out. When they were children, Eva would sit on Josephine's father's leg and wind his watch and glide her hand down his forearm to watch the hair rise under her touch. Perched on the other thigh, Josephine gave her dark looks, silently ordering her to release her father, who should have been worshiped from a distance, like a god or a blinding light. But Eva ignored her and, one day, seeing that her father was amused rather than annoyed by all the frolic, Josephine put a hand on his cheek and pinched, pulled his nose and ears and continued her groping even though he was now looking at her with surprise, while Eva, having stopped her own explorations, smiled mockingly. Josephine's cheeks burned, yet she was unstoppable, growing bolder to hide her awkwardness. She took his glasses and ran away with them, stumbling against the furniture. Without his glasses, her father could barely see, but it was as if she were the one deprived of sight, blindly reaching for a hiding place, shrieking with false joy, wishing he would hurry up and catch her. It was Eva who caught her and locked her in her arms and pushed her kicking and screaming toward him. Josephine felt her cousin's hot triumph singe the back of her neck. She released her father's glasses into his hand where they fell limply. Without taking his eyes off her, he ordered her to her room where she lay sobbing. Later Eva came to her and rocked her in her arms. "Silly!" she said. "You should have known when to stop."

All Josephine had done was copy her cousin and it had backfired. But oh, she couldn't imagine her life without Eva. She was nothing without her. Yet in Josephine's dreams, Eva was grateful and deferential, for she was the poor relative and Josephine's father was superior to hers, a simple mechanic who drank and could barely write his name.

Josephine could not forgive her for joining the Christian militia. More than anything, Josephine's father had hated parochialism. Eva had sat in their living room for hours listening to him. At least in this, in her father, Josephine had been Eva's superior. After he died, Eva showed her true colors, and Josephine felt rebuked. The brief affair later, that crazy, crazy thing (what was Eva thinking?) between Eva and George did not matter as much. Eva was a flirt and poor George was inexperienced, and Josephine and her mother watched helplessly while she broke his heart. No, nothing was everlasting like that betrayal.

"Michel is dead."

It takes Josephine a few seconds to understand, and a few more to catch her breath. Michel?

"His car fell in the wadi."

The world spins, an icy hand grips her chest and squeezes and makes her, once the words, with their bitter caustic taste, have settled on her tongue and in the back of her throat, reach for the orange drops on her nightstand and pour them in her mouth like medicine.

She doesn't know why she must react so strongly to the news. She can't even remember Michel's face clearly. Pieces of a memory she scrambles to glue together: the glint of a smile on perfect teeth, coarse black hair, puffiness around the eyes, perhaps from drinking too much. Even when she was there, she saw him like that, in fragments, and in his colors and textures, in the shadows that outlined his features, as if she had no time for the details of lips and nose and eyes, and no curiosity at all about the shape of his hands or ears. She'd had no desire to know him, really. Briefly, they were stealing kisses in the car and behind trees, having sex on dead leaves. She was leaving for the States soon and she could get away with breaking the rules. But her interest waned as the date of their departure grew near, as if Michel were extra luggage she'd rather not take along with her. Poor Michel. She had been cruel to him. And now he is dead.

Michel's death matters. Because she wants the land she left to remain unchanged, her memories of it untainted. Because change necessitates a reevaluation, and now she has despaired of meaning. But most of all, because every time she thought of Lebanon she had felt herself loved. Perhaps Michel loved her until the day he died. And now he is gone.

After they hang up, Josephine remembers how in Beirut she used to walk by parked cars and imagine them exploding. She thought she knew how it felt to die that way: first the deafening sound, then one leapt into a blinding, fractured light. She closes her eyes and imagines this over and over. In her fantasy, the dead relive that moment constantly, but they can't see what happens after the light; they live in the ignorance of their own destruction. In knowing, they would cease to exist. What keeps them from complete dissolution is their inability to cross the threshold of the first moment of the blast, that explosion that cancels, with its terrible light, the last horrible gasp.

Poor, poor Michel.

THE TROUBLE WITH THE WAR, she thinks, drowning the parsley in a bowl of water, was she couldn't see her flowers behind the sandbags. Farid was the one who planted the gardenia and the jasmine. After he'd finished patting the earth, he looked up at her. "Think where they'll be in ten years," he said, shading his face from the sun. Ten years sure seemed like a long time to the youths they were. She took his hand and helped him up. Together they admired their new garden. Yes, they thought, their lives would be as luminous as this morning in the sun.

He was a good dancer, Farid. Skipping down the dance floor of that restaurant in the mountains they loved to frequent before the children were born, the doors opening when the weather was hot onto a patio with eucalyptus trees and bougainvillea. They were like birds briefly alight for an embrace then taking off, spinning under the open sky.

Emilie gives the parsley a second bath and takes a peek at the leg of lamb, cooking nicely in its juices. She chops the onion and parsley. Kafta wasn't on the menu. She cranes her neck to listen. No sign of Salma. She looks for a place to hide the meat should her daughter-in-law come in and find her in the act. Taking her courage in both hands, she kneads the parsley and onion into the ground meat and adds salt and pepper.

Later, when the storm lets up, she will bring him some kafta.

ALL SUMMER AT THAT BEACH she had read, and once in a while she had caught Uncle Farid looking at her. And because of his eyes on her, trying to break into, she thought, her secret self, she imagined herself full of wonderful possibilities. She was the Chosen One, the wondrous child who would blossom into her destiny. She wouldn't have done it if he hadn't looked at her that way, as if she had already been forgiven for all her trespasses.

He had returned her kiss, of that she was sure. She felt his lips giving in, pressing down on hers, his desire for more. Then it was over. He moved away abruptly while she stood trembling. She saw him as if through a thick fog, the sun streaming from the window behind his back and making him appear as if he were not standing only a few feet away from her but far away, an impossible distance. She heard him indistinctly as he said what they had done was wrong. That it should never happen again. He left her standing in the middle of the room she was sharing with Josephine, in the house they had rented for the summer. She locked the door and hid under the covers to relive the kiss, elated and terrified of what she had done, what he must now think of her. Had she not thrown herself at him, had she not, when he came into the room looking for Josephine, slowly walked up to him, her eyes locked on his, and raised herself to him? The next several days she pretended to be ill so she could stay in her room. Then her fever became real. In her hallucinations, she saw herself adopted by him and her aunt Emilie, who was not her real aunt in those dreams but a beautiful and glamorous stranger who bestowed love and knowledge.

And then they died. Her uncle and her mother. She was relieved that her aunt had been spared, for she had wished for her aunt's death so that she might devote her entire life to him, and for this she was ashamed. With him gone, their kiss was buried forever away in a grave by the mountainside.

Their death was convenient. That was her first thought, and because of this she had more to forgive herself for than a brief and forbidden infatuation. They died and she felt herself saved. The way she felt later, surviving the war even though she was right in the middle, not fighting but taking care of the fighters, cleaning, feeding them. And she had gotten away with it, the way she had gotten away with that kiss and her uncle died so she wouldn't have to look in his eyes, and her mother followed him so she wouldn't have to look in her eyes. But now perhaps it was time for payback. Perhaps. What was that American saying and why did she remember it now? The chickens have come home to roost. But hasn't she paid enough? No one knew anything and of course it was crazy and it had been that one quick kiss, so innocent when you thought of all the kisses she has given and received since. But sometimes she thought there must have been more than one kiss, something awful she had suppressed, like those people who shut out bad memories and discovered them by accident one day while watering the garden. Her fantasies ran freely. She imagined herself molested as a child by that janitor in their building who always looked up her skirt when she climbed the stairs.

But she knew none of it was true. Life was traumatizing enough without having to invent your horror stories. Your husband lay on the snow in a pool of blood. The violence became an everyday occurrence even without the bombs. It seethed inside you. You flared up at the least inconvenience. People killed each other over parking spots. And once in a while, she still thought of that kiss, which had meant the beginning of something, the loss of her innocence. How about him, her uncle? Did he make up his mind to die? Did he slam into that truck on purpose? The arrogance of this thought, she scolds herself. He was so much older. She has no sense of proportion. So you think a kiss one afternoon had turned him suicidal? That kiss dislodged something in her, an obstruction that had kept her until that day on the straight and narrow, a prize pupil and a good girl. She stayed chaste, all right, but at what price, scrubbing off that kiss with bathroom cleaner, taunting then rejecting the men who flocked to her door. Then Robert died and something else got unclogged. Sometimes she imagined she had caused her cousins' and aunt's exile. She remembered her aunt approaching her in a roundabout way, telling her how she hated the thought of going to the United States. Eva had changed the subject.

After Robert died, she often thought of morality, her mother's influence probably, and how much she yearned for fortitude and wished for her life to be different, and yet she did everything in her power to scoff at conventions.

She broke George's heart and still they forgave her. And that she couldn't bear, because it confirmed what they thought of her, the poor relative who couldn't control her actions. She would be forgiven because her lot in life was so small in comparison. She had burrowed in their lives like a small needy animal and made herself the center of their desires, and still she had been perfectly expendable. George looked at her with longing and she liked seeing him want her and suffer for it. She had lain in bed for hours thinking about it. She had imagined him, her uncle, on top of her. This oneness with him she craved with all her soul. Yet when he died, racked with guilt, she had broken George's heart. Still, they forgave her.

THE BAG WHERE SHE HAS PACKED the kafta tugs at Emilie's wrist. She keeps her head bowed against the wind and looks up once in a while to spot the mound. She took off without a plan. There he was, atop his wall, and because she could see him from her window, the journey, all of it—the wind, the blinding whiteness, the possibility of rejection—had seemed conquerable. Yet in the time it took her to get dressed for the trip and elude questions (not a hard feat, her family firmly retreated into their individual chambers), he had disappeared. Gone inside, where normal people should be during a blizzard. Yet she lumbers on without losing heart, for there is kafta to deliver, a trail to break.

In front of the house, she skirts a silhouette on the ground. Flapping her wings like a beautiful angel. She hears Shirin chuckling. Talking about angels? You?

Her sister's white hair lay loose on the pillow. All her life, Emilie hated that coil on her sister's head, hated the small round heads of the pins sticking out from it. They were like thorns (Shirin's crown of thorns), the depth of their thrust a conjecture. Later, when Shirin's hair turned gray, those pins made her think of dead flies floating in a cloudy broth. An image more benign than thorns but still troubling, as if her sister had left behind solid flesh to enter a watery, murky world. And then the loose hair on the pillow, like something private laid out for her scrutiny. She couldn't avert her eyes. There were none of the knots and gnarls that Emilie had imagined under her sister's tight bun all these years, only thin ropes of gray hair spread across the white sheets and giving off a faintly briny scent. Emilie remembered seeing the coil getting smaller, a single pin holding it together in the end, while her own hair remained a luxuriant mane despite only the one year separating the sisters. In a fit of guilt, she realized that she had not given it another thought, had not wondered at the discrepancy.

When Shirin died, color took over her body: pale blue and gray, the green of bruises and swamps. She was transformed, Shirin but not Shirin.

In no time, Emilie is soaking wet, frozen to the bone. A wool coat and wool shawl wound around her head not the best of attire. Her feet, although still dry in her good boots, have lost all sensitivity.

She wades on, her memories no longer a hedge against loss but loss itself.

Yussef, too, had been half kin and half stranger. Josephine has his thick eyebrows. Like him, her thumbs are eerily flexible, bending all the way back to her wrists. He gave Emilie little presents to take home, licorice, coins, wrappers, buttons, orange peel, anything he found when the thought suddenly hit him, as it did every day at the same time she got ready to leave, and always as if for the first time, that she shouldn't be allowed to leave empty-handed. He folded her fingers over his treasures, and she did her best not to recoil. They were always small things that seemed to have come out of an intimate part of him, a place that was childlike and needy but also slightly revolting. She didn't see them then as she would later, the first communication from a life until then under lock and key. She went to his apartment and scrubbed and cleaned, and came out feeling happy with herself and rushed home to wash. It wouldn't do, now, after all this time, to ask for forgiveness.

Yussef was blood kin, and still she and Farid believed the worst. Said, "What has the world come to? See how evil springs from your closest kin? After everything we have done for him." Poor Yussef, who was mad and couldn't help himself. "But what were we supposed to do?" they asked each other. Locked him away in an institution and came home to raise their daughter, and never from that day on looked each other in the eyes without seeing that flicker pass quickly like a flash in the dark, a flicker of guilt or uncertainty or relief, that they had finally put him away, that they would no longer have to hide him, that Josephine, and later George, would not know him. That they might not have to wonder what brings a man to the edge and leaves him there to die.

They thought evil came from the most surprising places, but all the while they knew evil was the wrong word for what happened. Or maybe when it came from blood kin, evil lost its clarity, was muddled and diluted by all the other things Yussef was.

Evil too strong a word for what poor Yussef did. She saw him bolt out of the kitchen after he had laid his hands on her shoulder, saw him in the living room holding Josephine and those eyes fixed on her baby like they had the power to set her on fire, and she must have hit him with something because he almost dropped Josephine but she plucked her from him and ran out the door. Only much later did she wonder about Yussef's eyes and how they might have been filled not with madness but with infinite love.

She stopped believing in evil after that. At least in her ability to recognize it. The war came and she tended her garden and waited for the madness to fade. Didn't believe in evil any more than she believed the war was going to last forever. It was bound to burn itself out, to go back where it came from.

Some things you never leave behind. They become one with you and you aren't aware that you are carrying them within until something tells you to look inside. The snow blanketing the earth. Eva coming. The interruption of her exchange with their neighbor. She is trudging through a blizzard to take food to a neighbor who might or might not give her an exquisite wooden statue for it. The wind and the snow batter her face. But in the distance she thinks she sees the sky open, and out comes an orange light to seep through the skeletons of trees and collect on the ground in shimmering pools and flit and flicker and burn through the total whiteness until the colors underneath are finally revealed. Delivered of their weight, the slender trees bend with the wind, and the colossal oaks seem to darken and cling to the earth with renewed vigor.

And in that light, she sees Eva crying by the window, looking up at the overcast sky. It was a chilly day, the coldest day of the year, the entire winter a record cold that year, but no snow because it never snows in Beirut. The rain pours and the sky thunders and the wind blows something fierce, but it doesn't snow. Imagine being back in Beirut. The cars, the cart vendors, a world of noise and constant little causes for irritation, a world without snow. Would the rain have carved her skin differently, found other places to erode? Would her memories have stayed sharp, constantly replenished and kept alive by new ones, the old faces still like new? Or, on the contrary, would the bounty have made her complacent, indifferent toward what was easy to come by?

Eva crying on the day of her mother's funeral, standing against the window, the pale light of that morning outlining her silhouette. She was in mourning, her neck emerging delicately from her thin body. Her right hand clutched the curtain and her left one rested on the windowsill. Her body gently shook with her sobbing. Emilie raised her arm to her niece's shoulder, but before she could touch her, a car honked. Eva dried her tears and turned around to leave. She looked surprised to find her aunt there, her arm suspended in midair. In her niece's eyes, Emilie saw defiance. She would go out to meet that man even though her mother's body was still warm and unburied. She would learn to forget, to quickly shake away unhappiness. What else could she do? What lessons could be learned from a mother's death? And yet this immediate hurling toward life and pleasure! Emilie sunk her fingers in her niece's arm. Eva let out a cry and Emilie released her and she was gone.

Eva and Josephine knew so little outside the war. Grew up thinking the land was so evil they had to run from it. There was nothing evil about the land. It was just as good and bountiful as it had been before the war, you just had to dig for it harder, that's all, but the goodness was still there, like the bulbs Emilie planted every fall, hard and tight as eggs, blooming every spring.

And it is a giant egg, this snow. You must dig harder for the beauty, that's all.

Thoughts rattle in her head. Pebbles is how she thinks of them, beach-smoothed pebbles in a pail between George and Josephine who are scooping sand in then scooping it out in red pails, and her husband reading his paper behind his sunglasses, and once in a while she is touched by anxiety at the thought of Yussef. How sorry she is he isn't here to share this vacation with them, and in the same breath she is relieved of all the cooking and cleaning, relieved that for the last several years someone else has been in charge, someone faceless in a government asylum far inside the city.

And Eva sitting slightly on the side, keeping her distance. ⌟ toes in the sand. Closing her eyes in the sun, waiting. Emilie can ⌐ niece's thoughts, although she would do anything not to be able to.

Waiting: waiting out the storm, waiting out a battle. She got tired ⌐ waiting, that's all. She left to bring a little kafta to their neighbor, and to ask him why he stopped leaving her wooden statues.

Waiting until her husband and her niece came to their senses. Until they wiped that kiss clean off their lips. Until she could no longer feel the quiver of their hunger. And so she leaned back in her chair and looked out at the sea, and wished for the first time in her life that she could leave forever.

She walks, her legs sinking in the snow, toward the cream-colored house with the dark green shutters, toward the snow mountain, and that world that she is about to touch.

IT WAS MEAN, downright cruel of her, but Salma couldn't help it. She had been doing pretty well up until then, keeping her mouth shut and going about her business despite the two blights that, today of all days, stranded as she was in the house, deeply affronted her sense of harmony and purpose: her daughter's sloth and her mother-in-law's sloppiness in the kitchen. In the living room, George surfed the channels with his remote, and she had silently fussed, the fussing a way to distract herself from thinking about the mess her mother-in-law was making in the kitchen. Crumbs and stains made her crazy. A sink full of dirty dishes was devastating. Never was she happier than on the eve of a major cleanup, thinking ahead to the lavender to be sprinkled on the linen, its perfume drifting to the dark corners where cobwebs had hung and been swiftly removed. George finally settled on a channel, and she stood up and headed back to the kitchen, bracing herself for what she might discover.

Everything was clean when she made her entrance. Yet her delight was short-lived. Before she'd had a chance to scold herself for her hasty condemnation (all Emilie had wanted was to lend a hand), before she could enjoy the sight of a kitchen free from detritus, a kitchen orderly and disinfected from any traces of living matter, before she could let her eyes travel down the spread of spotless counters and sink and floor where, had the sun been shining today, it would have illuminated and enhanced the cleanliness and filled her heart with pleasure; before any of this could occur, there was her mother-in-law greedily licking her fingers, a big mound of kafta in the bowl in front of her speckled with parsley and mint and spices and onion, and Emilie sticking one finger then the other in her mouth in an odious torrent of sucking and slurping. Salma waited expectantly. Surely Emilie will wash her hands? But the fingers plunged back into the meat and kneaded. Salma's cheeks burned. "Shouldn't you have washed your hands first?" she blurted.

Emilie's face switched from surprise to sadness, and finally to a resignation that made Salma lower her eyes. Yet, try as she might (and she did try to convince herself that the damage was reversible, that the heat would purify), she couldn't chase away the image of her mother-in-law's saliva penetrating the meat. (Although kafta hadn't been on the menu, but Salma *sympathy* lets this slide.) Her old woman's secretions, a faint whiff of urine and stale sweat always about her seeping through to everything she touched. Salma couldn't help it. The threat of germs undercut her best intentions, made her ruthless.

Emilie washed her hands and started making the patties. Salma inched closer and washed the bowl. Said things smelled divine. Lingered, busying herself, pretending to check on the leg of lamb. Emilie left the kitchen as soon as the patties were in the oven, and Salma returned to the living room.

There, she inhaled deeply, as if the smoke from George's cigarette would sweep her mind clear of her latest blunder, and turned her attention to him. Her husband, salt of the earth, who was bound, if she knew him at all, to do something to annoy and distract her from worrying about her mother-in-law. They were losing money and it will be hard to recover. This will make him ill-tempered for a while. He will ask for restitution, meals on time, coffee in his thermos. The TV spewed out the usual bad news. A girl abducted from her bedroom. A bomb exploding outside an abortion clinic. Love had once welled in her chest. What happens later? Is it exile that breaks up a marriage, drives a wedge between two people? Each of them too busy cobbling up a life from scratch to mind the other?

He never told her his true thoughts about being here. This land has bounty, he liked to say. It was her only indication that he was grateful. She didn't know if he was happy. He tried to keep up with the events back home. Every bit of news after their departure, the escalation of the war, the failing economy, the Israeli and Syrian occupations, proved he had been right to leave. Only Marie caused him to doubt his judgment, this stubborn girl who behaved like a boy. Half the time he didn't know what she was up to.

Salma knew what Marie was up to. Prying was a mother's prerogative, and she snooped regularly in her daughter's room. Just the other day she had found an application to a university in California. Her daughter was always scheming, always wanting more. Leaving a perfectly good job at McDonald's because she couldn't stand how her hair smelled at the end of the day. Getting another job at a flower shop with lower pay and fewer hours.

Salma tilted back in her chair, wondering when exactly her daughter intended to break the news. Who did she think was going to fork out the thousands for her to attend a university on the other side of the country? Her eyes wandered back to the TV screen. George had switched to a local station. This was the worst storm Vermont had seen in decades. Tractors were plowing the streets. The snow would later be dumped in the river, the only place left, with the high precipitation they'd seen this year. Snow banks had become a hazard. Would her neighbor have to tear down his mound of snow? She hoped not, although she knew that soon, something, the sun or a snowplow, would get the better of it, the way one thing or another always got the better of refuge.

It was George who first noticed Emilie's absence. "Where is Mother?" he asked. She was used to him asking this question the moment he returned from the store and a few more times during the course of the evening, and she usually answered without trying to conceal her irritation. The older woman spent her days between the kitchen and the living room, sparing her legs the journey to the second floor until bedtime. I stuffed her in the freezer. I fed her to the pigeons. Salma didn't say these things, but it gave her some relief to think them.

She knew why he asked. How he worried it was a matter of time before his mother took off again the way she would back in Beirut, disappearing for hours without bothering to tell anyone where she was going. Had to have her dose of fresh air while a war raged on. And her children, whose peace of mind she discounted, although grown by then, were still dependent on their mother, still clinging to her, too spineless to demand, if not that she put a stop to her walks, then that she at least provide them with an itinerary. The two of them would sit by the

126

window and wait for her return, Josephine rapping her knuckles on the table, George pacing.

When George asked Salma his question today, she did not answer with her usual flippancy, which sounded an alarm for him. "She left the kitchen a short while ago," she said demurely, which made him get up to look in the kitchen and the living room, then come back to announce with panic in his voice that his mother was in neither. Together they searched for her, George looking at Salma with suspicion. On hearing the commotion, Josephine joined the search, eyeing them both quizzically. When it was clear that Emilie was not in the house, Salma told them about the incident in the kitchen.

"Surely asking her to wash her hands . . ." she demurred.

"God, woman," her husband said.

So it had happened again. Eighteen years had not changed Emilie, and the blizzard had not stopped her any more than the bombs had at one time from simply leaving when the fancy took her. But she was a lot older now. She was probably lost and cold in a strange place. And it was all Salma's fault.

"She couldn't have gone far," she said. Brother and sister briefly nodded. Josephine stared at her stonily.

She didn't offer to accompany them. After their departure, she stood in the foyer with her hands drawn into her armpits. Surely she had not asked for much, only a bit of healthful and godly sanitation. But she had done enough damage for one day. She'd stay put and tend to things until everyone's safe return, and perhaps by then all would have been forgiven. Feeling better, she went looking for Marie and sank to the floor and started to weep when she couldn't find her daughter. A few minutes later, Marie walked in. "Just where the hell have you been?" Salma yelled, springing to her feet.

"I was outside. I got sick of staying in my room. Is that against the law? God, what's wrong with you?"

Fury shot through her. Salma drew breath, and in a quick rattle she fired at her astounded daughter the bitterness of the last few years. She knew that Marie was ashamed of them, she knew about her secret plans to go to California. And halfway through, she slipped in the incident in the kitchen.

"Jesus, Mother. Can't you at least try?"

Once again, she stood accused. This time she would defend herself. But before she'd uttered a word, her daughter had disappeared. Salma waited for the usual numbness to envelop her. It couldn't get any worse than this. Her mother-in-law was in grave danger and her family wasn't talking to her. She went to the kitchen to make coffee and drank it standing at the sink, staring at the air around her. After she washed her cup, she dressed warmly and walked out into the blizzard after her family.

JOSEPHINE STAGGERS BEHIND GEORGE. The gusting wind blinds her and she keeps her eyes on her brother's red scarf. She grabbed Marie's ski goggles before leaving the house, but she forgot to bring a scarf and her cheeks sting with the cold. A glance at her watch tells her they have been out a short while and must still be in their front yard, yet she feels as if they have been roaming for hours without direction, the sky low above them and the silence complete but for the howling wind. The snow gets in her mouth and nose. She imagines being swollen with it. She remembers the stuffed owl she once bought from a fair. She had been able to keep it a few short hours before her aunt secretly tossed it in the trash when they stopped for refreshments, casting out bad luck. It had been a second-rate job, the skin gaping at the seams. The owl sacrificed for this. And yet the wings silky and surprisingly strong, as if they'd kept something of their former power. A shell of its past self, what it had once been now completely obliterated, except for the strange and sad vigor of these wings.

Instinctively they walk toward Loom's house. Every once in a while, the wind dies down to let them see the dark shutters and the brick chimney. She feels a surge of gratitude whenever the snow mound appears, as if it is calling on them to keep going even though her mother's tracks are gone, wiped out by the wind and fresh snow.

Still, doubt. Her heart sinking at the thought. What if they don't find her? The snow up to their knees, and her mother buried in it. She might be near and yet they can't see her. It will take a great melting before they uncover her poor frozen body. Josephine calls her brother's name. "We'll find her," he replies, and she wants to believe him more than anything.

Loom's mound flashes again. Their houses are set on the diagonal. She has watched him long enough from her window to remember every landmark: The two pine trees set a few feet from the entrance, the old carriage wheel he put there when he moved in. Everything is covered with snow, but she has her memory to guide her.

It's all they have to go on but it is something, and for this reason she carries on.

For a moment she can't see George. Time stands still and she is a hard core without past or future, frozen in the present, the snow wrapping her in its brilliant eternity. The threat of never seeing her mother again fading before the irresistible pull of the snow, her knees bending to sink in it, breathless against the wind and the cold, feeling herself beginning to cry. She should have done something, paid more attention, coaxed her mother into talking. How could she have let herself forget how, in Beirut, her mother would disappear and return hours later to resume her life among them without explanation, to cook and clean and, when she had the inclination, sit down to knit as if nothing had happened? When they moved to the States, Josephine convinced herself that her mother would be too scared to venture out into a strange land, and Josephine was thankful to have her mother safely at home, even as the older woman wilted and shrunk before her eyes. They had all grown smaller somehow. Going to the store and back is all they do. Their lives, their dreams, shrunken.

The wind carries George's voice back to her and the blood flows in her veins again and she moves forward, toward the red scarf and his voice calling her name.

27

IN HER HOTEL ROOM IN NEW YORK, Eva knows something is wrong when no one answers her calls. She has lost count of how many times she's already phoned her aunt and cousin in the few hours since her landing. She could be using her time better, getting a little sleep to shake off jet lag or whiling away the time at the hotel's magazine stand and a perfume shop where she could be getting a head start on her shopping for friends and Marietta back home. But here she is, fretting about getting no answer when it's been less than an hour since they last talked. In Lebanon, months would go by without a word, and now this compulsion to keep talking.

Testing the waters, exploring where they stand after years of separation. Provoking something—this? Whatever it is, this foreboding in her chest. Yes, something is surely wrong.

28

DAVID RECOGNIZED HER RIGHT AWAY. Clad in dark but barely visible, engulfed by whiteness. When she started to walk in circles, he yelled at her to stand still and ran out.

In the living room, he helped her take off her coat and put on his bathrobe. He brought warm water in a basin and proceeded to take off her socks, but she pushed him away and pulled her socks off herself. When her feet entered the hot water, she winced. He stood back, watching her relax, a thawing he could almost feel in his own body. He motioned for her to put her hands in the water and knead at her feet. She put down the plastic bag she had been clutching on the seat next to her and did as he instructed.

After she had dried herself, he gave her hot chocolate and motioned for her to lie down. She picked up the bag that smelled of meat and onion and gave it to him. Then she lay down and closed her eyes.

She looked so small and old it was a miracle she had survived the walk. He chuckled when he opened the bag, and instantly his eyes watered. He had been living on canned food, hot chocolate and cigarettes for days, and Myra would have done just that: would have offered him food immediately she saw him.

Now this woman probably expected a statue in return. He had stopped leaving them in the clearing. In the beginning, it seemed like a good way to make gifts of Myra's creations. Then, worried it might turn into a long-term exchange, he had stopped.

She stared at him. He shifted from one to foot to the other and tried to explain that it was his wife who had made the statues, that he himself was not artistic in the least. She continued to look at him without understanding. Finally he brought a picture of his wife and son taken at a ski resort, pulled out Husky's statue from his pocket and pointed at his wife. At last, she seemed to grasp what he was trying to tell her and looked around.

He explained that they were dead. He told her about the accident. How he had been at the office when it happened, how he allowed one of his colleagues to drive him to the hospital because he was already breaking into pieces. He didn't care if she couldn't understand a word he said. She leaned against the pillow and looked at him. Finally he stopped talking and sat in a chair, waiting for someone to claim her.

While she slept, he looked at a picture of his wife and son on the table. Myra had not been a classical beauty. Her chin jutted and she hated the loose skin on her neck that started appearing in her thirties. And yet he had fallen head over heels the first time he saw her, sitting in the seat in front of him in music theory class, turning around to pass him a handout. No one had smiled at him like that before.

He wished someone would hurry up and come for the older woman. He wanted to get back to his igloo.

It wasn't long before they started trickling in. The man and the woman, brother and sister, followed by the man's wife and his daughter. They spoke in broken English, except for the young girl. As soon as they entered the house, the brother and his sister rushed to their mother and inspected her. The man thanked him effusively, and David almost stopped him in midsentence to tell him he hadn't had a choice in the matter. As a matter of fact, he would very much appreciate it if they'd hurry up and take the older woman home. But immediately he saw Myra frowning and felt obligated to offer hospitality and hot chocolate. The man's sister offered to help but he declined. They seemed embarrassed, unsure what to do next. The young girl paced back and forth. If Brendan had lived, she might have babysat him. His stomach knotted at the thought. If Myra were here, she would have teased out their story despite the language barrier. She would have sat with them and soothed and commiserated.

When he came back with the hot chocolate, they were still standing where he had left them, looking at the older woman who slept unaware. He took his seat beside the fire and threw in a new log. No one spoke. In silence they stood, waiting for her to wake up and tell them why they had gathered here under his roof. Grudgingly, he felt that some meaning might yet come out of this. Here: a family. He shuddered with the frailty of it. He saw the cracks despite the way they sat close together. How vulnerable they seemed, despite all that they had, life, family, good intentions. They waited patiently for her to waken. And in this, the probability of her awakening, they had been spared. Which was more than anyone could hope for.

STRANGE TO BE HERE, in Loom's living room. For what remains after
their initial frenzied arrival at his door, their storming in and relief at
finding their mother sleeping on the couch, their thorough but quiet (she
looked so restful in her sleep) inspection of her body, their effusive expres-
sions of gratitude to Loom for taking her in (at which he looked slightly
bored), what remains after all that is the strangeness of it, the disquiet-
ing, thrilling feeling that they have been catapulted outside the edges of
their existence and into this scarcely furnished room, the fire burning in
the fireplace, the dog-eared books on the mantle, and the floor-to-ceiling
wood paneling, the only touch of luxury that must, she imagines, she
doesn't know why, vex Loom, or in the very least leave him indifferent,
for this is how Josephine sees him, impatient with superfluity, contemptu-
ous of anything but an honest barrenness.

Like a wave, they roll back together to one side of the only sofa where
the older woman sleeps under a red blanket. George, Salma, Marie, and
Josephine, standing in a row, eyeing the fall and rise of the older woman's
chest, the light tilt of her head on the white pillow, the general happy sinking of her body into the velvet cushions. Josephine knows what Salma and
George are thinking, as if suddenly they are all one in this stranger's house:
Salma's longing for the one free chair by the fire, George's confusion in light
of Loom's unresponsiveness. Should he offer compensation in the form of
a lifetime supply of groceries? Invite him to dinner and pledge his eternal
gratitude? Josephine senses their bewilderment, their tongues trussed, the
words failing them in the face of this wonder: their mother sleeping peacefully on this stranger's couch. Should she wake up and refuse to leave, they

will bow to her wishes and go back home, dumbfounded and silent, and mark today as the day their mother finally broke away.

Did she imagine him speaking earlier (now he sits silently in one of the two chairs by the fire, looking at nothing in particular), the words almost too slow for his lips, something unsynchronized between the sound and sight of him, or was it some maladjustment in her own brain which was unable to take in the whole picture at once? He explains how he first heard her mother crying for help outside the mound, how he instructed her to take off her wet socks and soak her feet in warm water, how she fell asleep immediately upon hitting the couch. The image of her mother wandering the edge of his mound, wildly digging her fingers into the snow, briefly steals her breath, but quickly Josephine is folded into the raspy percolations of his voice, and she knows that from now on she will always want to be near him.

He doesn't go out of his way to play the gracious host, although he is not in the least rude. He seems to recognize that they came together under peculiar circumstances indeed but he would wait it out, he would see it through with them wherever it might take him. But in the meantime, he isn't wasting time on small talk and niceties. Except to stand up all of a sudden and offer hot chocolate, which they gratefully accept, and then turn her down, but not unkindly, when she offers to help.

When he's gone, she summons him back in her mind to take stock: in his mid-forties, on the short side but well-built and moving with enough confidence to appear taller. Still wearing his hat, so no way of knowing the color of his hair. Judging from his skin it must be on the dark side, although how can one be sure? It irks her, this secrecy about his hair, this inflated importance accorded to it, so that he feels the need to hide it from scrutiny, to elude exposure. Perhaps his refusal to let her help him with the chocolate had stung more than she realized.

He returns with four steaming mugs on a tray and a plastic container with a stack of kafta patties. He explains they are from her mother, that she has been leaving him food for weeks. It is quite all right, he adds when he sees their shock, he is utterly grateful, he isn't much of a cook himself and is tired of eating KFC and grilled steaks.

Time weighs unequally: entire years can leave a smaller impact than a single moment.

Josephine begins by counting: her mother is sixty-nine when you do the math, a little more than two decades older than Josephine. Her mother was younger than Josephine is now when she lost her husband. Will Josephine step one day into the same puddle of time and understand what drove her mother out into the storm to bring food to a stranger?

Her mother's coat is draped on the chair facing Loom. Josephine walks over and picks it up, then folds it carefully and sits uninvited.

Salma takes her lead from Josephine and squeezes down on the sofa next to her mother-in-law, who is still sleeping.

"I am Josephine Zaydan," she says, her hand extended. He is David Finch. Now she must stop calling him Loom. Now he has a name, and she must contend with that.

Marie sits unceremoniously on the floor between them and begins to talk. Josephine knows the young girl is about to reveal how they had been watching him for months from their window, how they started calling him Loom one day on a whim, and she stops her with a glare. Marie changes course but doesn't stop talking. She wants to know why he spends so much time outside, if he has a job, if he's been overseas. Loom looks beset. "Please stop," Josephine says, but it is too late. Loom has asked to be excused.

"Nice going," she says when he's gone. The bitterness in her voice surprises even her. Marie shrugs and lies on her stomach, staring at the fire. Salma takes the chair vacated by Loom. By David, Josephine corrects herself. She offers her chair to George and moves to the couch next to her mother. Like playing musical chairs, she thinks, except no one gets left out.

Her mother's coat is still folded in her lap. Look at it, she tells herself. Look at it closely, the way a child bends down to inspect the ants scurrying near his feet, and leaves the world with a sweep. But instead, she looks away and around her.

It is really pleasant here, the fire burning, her mother's breathing now the only sound in the room, George, Salma, and Marie looking lovely and pink-cheeked by the fire, for once not fighting or snapping at each other. Is this happiness, this stillness, this absence of discord? But why must happiness be an absence? She looks around for David who has escaped in a hurry, away from Marie who breathed over his shoulder, prodding, questioning, demanding to know. How can she look at her mother's coat after that? Why not let her keep her secrets?

Yet she imagines that her mother is allowing her this dance of her hands down the wide collar of her coat, brushing off the hair and dust on the back, straightening the arms and pulling down at the hem, emptying the pockets and trying to reclaim, through these simple gestures, the familiarity that her mother, by taking off in a storm to bring food to a stranger, has shattered.

When mothers stray, the world stops.

Nothing happens. The coat does not reveal her mother's secrets.

Her mother stirs, opening her eyes, finding Josephine's. Josephine presses a finger to her lips and Emilie nods. She doesn't want them descending on her with their questions.

"What got into you?" she whispers, smiling, letting her mother know she is not angry.

Emilie says Eva's name. Josephine shakes her head. No news. She waves her hand at the window to signify the snow hasn't let up yet.

In all the commotion following her mother's disappearance, she has forgotten about Eva. Here her cousin seems unreal, as if they have stepped into another world. Her mother has done that. She has pulled them away, plucked them out in her wake.

When their mother would disappear in Beirut, George and Josephine would stand at the window looking out at the sky, as if they could predict the likelihood of a battle that day, as if the war had entered the cosmos and become one with the weather. When their mother returned, she would not reveal where she had gone, and they would hover in the kitchen while she prepared dinner, afraid to ask questions, fluctuating between anger and curiosity.

All their lives, she was steady as a rock: there all the time, when you woke up and when you went to sleep. But they sensed she would do exactly as she pleased if it was important enough for her. She would sacrifice only after careful thought, and only when sacrifice was absolutely called for.

Her parents owed their marriage to her mother. She was at the oars steering, and without her they would have floundered and lost their course. In many ways, she was conventional: a homemaker, believing in family and obligations. Her rebellions were enough to define her, ever: she did not believe in God, was outspoken against the war, and not care in the least about being a good housekeeper.

Eva tried hard to impress Josephine's father but it was Josephine's mother she sought, plopping herself on a chair while they rolled grape leaves or shelled peas. Josephine's father was always teaching and making a good use of their time, but her mother took one in simply, didn't ask for anything in return but the courtesy of being companionable for the lapse of time they happened to share. She made the best of what she was dealt (her lack of formal education, the fact that she could barely read and write) and did not allow her learned husband and his friends to belittle her.

Her small rebellions. They do not count for much in this country. Here, her powers, faced with greater forces, with bigger milestones, shrunk. What did it matter, the courage it took to stand her ground, to tell the world she knew so much despite her illiteracy? Here, her accomplishments seemed little compared with what had been undertaken. People went farther every day. Her mother, taken out of her context, was suddenly less formidable, and the freedom she had daily wrested for herself appeared insignificant.

Freedom Josephine knew the last summer they spent in her mother's town before leaving for the United States. The sun was threading through the lemons hanging from the branches above. Above was also Michel's head with its thick, uncombed hair catching the spilling light. Vowing to love her until the day he died, although she was leaving in two short weeks. "I will love you until the day I die," he said, putting a hand on her chin and raising her lips to his. The day of his death seemed unimaginably distant then. He will soon forget her, she thought, while he lay beside her inconsolable and lonely, as if she had already left him.

He was secondary. The pleasure he gave her was not of his making alone. Because she was on the verge of leaving, it was possible to break the rules with impunity. Cautiously at first, because she knew traces of the old rules, some lingering fear of punishment or shame would follow her into the new world. Leaving wasn't dying, not entirely. But in the last few days before they left, she began to live in a constant state of exhilaration and lightheadedness, above conventions, as free as the wood animals that scurried around them and that she came to love with a new fondness. Although she was no lover of nature, she listened intently as Michel explained the potency of certain medicinal plants and the book he was planning to write. (Did it ever materialize?) Sometimes she loved him. How could she help it, when he had opened the curtains to this freedom? She could jump over a cliff and land unscathed. She dropped layers, became all body, all rebellion. And sometimes she forgot that it was Eva's husband she imagined lying on top of her; Robert, a man of the world, another one of Eva's prizes.

Then Eva came to visit with Robert, and Michel, with his uncombed hair and vague plans about writing a book, was eclipsed. Josephine stopped going to the lemon grove. It was only a week before she would be leaving for good, so what did a few days matter?

Was it self-punishment, this not looking at other men all these years? Or did things continue as before, the old fears alive still in the new order? The magic of the lemon grove unlocked only in the moment before leaving, when, on the brink of flight, one was freed and released into the altered world.

Now the scent of lemon is unbearable.

Her mother sits up, and instantly George and Salma have pounced upon her, feeling her forehead, brushing away her hair, propping up the pillows, George sitting by her side, Salma pacing back to the chair and sitting erect, her glances full of her readiness, now that Emilie was found, to face her punishment stoically, whatever it may be, for justice must be done, and she believes herself the cause of her mother-in-law's escape.

David reappears, wincing like someone who'd spent the last few hours in complete darkness and is now blinded by the bright light. He takes long steps towards the armchair by the fire and sits there without looking at them. It dawns on Josephine that this must be a daily occurrence for him, this reawakening to a new reality for which he must readjust after his brief escape. She sees him struggling against the tide of questions such as the ones Marie unleashed on him earlier, questions he must ask himself repeatedly. He carries about him an air of quest and disquiet, as if he goes through his days looking for the missing link that will set his mind at ease, and he seems to do so single-mindedly, pursuing one question under all the various guises it might take. She realizes this is where his kind of courage lies, in bringing himself back from the brink.

She leans back against the couch and contemplates him. He is handsome, she realizes with a start. He is handsome and she has missed her life.

He looks at her and she smiles. Once she was loved. Michel had loved her, and she thanks him silently for this even though she did not return his love, concluded that the mere fact he chose her to love made him unworthy. Such were the convolutions of her mind then, the sloppy, messy complications she couldn't wait to leave behind. And leave them behind she did, although, she realizes now, that is never truly possible. From a distance, Michel's love turned into a beautiful memory.

She has been loved. And with this, she smiles fully at David, as she must now call him.

EMILIE KNEW THEY WOULD FOLLOW HER and can't decide if she's relieved or irritated. When she had gone off in Beirut, roaming the streets, looking for she didn't know what, sometimes she had found small pieces of it, things she called Solitude, Peace, Rejuvenation, or simply Exercise, her body then more obliging, her joints well lubricated. She would walk for hours. The synergy was such between her brain and body that her feet simply took her outside and away whenever her mind got restless. It seemed that her best option was to trust and follow them, her feet, in their brisk, efficient stride. Pound pound flush. Her mind emptied, normal life resumed its course.

Earlier today, instead of pounding hard pavement, her feet sank in the snow. She trudged and fell, was blinded by the drift. Such silence suffusing her escape this time, such stumbling about. And yet, now she feels like jumping from the couch and hugging each and every one of them and crying, "I did it!"

She has rescued them all. Her heart wells up with tenderness.

Earlier, she had brushed them away angrily when they jumped on her with their questions. Now they are subdued and chastened, waiting for her to decide the next course of action. She loves them tremendously.

Her eyes are drawn to the fire in the middle of the dark room, the sparks a joyful celebration.

She smells the kafta she cooked this morning. He will have it for lunch.

She was never a good cook but Farid humored her. She knew he was lying when he exclaimed over her cooking, and she loved him for it.

He will eat her food and their exchange will resume. Yet without wooden statues this time, she remembers suddenly. His wife and child dead. Her heart squeezes with grief for him.

In the presence of death, it is harder to believe that life continues. That interruptions are momentary and the roads that fork eventually merge again. She feels the death of his wife and son fresh around her, his grief raw and awful.

Now she is full of sadness. She pounds at her legs that have carried her here and that now refuse to move. She feels herself a formless, shapeless lump again. Old and petty and superfluous. Yussef who wasted away at an asylum for wanting to lay his hand on her shoulder. Her husband kissing her niece. Eva coming. She realizes she has never entirely forgiven them. She realizes that, had she not bolted out of the apartment that day, she would have turned around and taken Yussef in her arms.

Perhaps she went out looking for goodness. Long ago she found it daily, when she looked from her balcony in Beirut at the dips and rises of the land, the mountains in the East, the sea stretching to the horizon. She missed her bird's-eye view, the feeling of being perched on the edge of infinity, of a whole world beyond herself, yet to which she felt closely linked. It made her seem good in her own eyes, this feeling of belonging. Worthy and upright.

And she has been, most of the time. When she lost track, it was tragic.

She looks down and finds that she is wearing his bathrobe.

"A good thing I don't have your fear of germs," she says to Salma, pointing at the clean but threadbare robe, smiling a little mischievously. A small victory, her shunning hygiene, but not at the expense of Salma, who sits up in her chair by the fire flattered, confirmed in her reputation of the queen of clean. No one dethroned, no one defeated in Emilie's triumph. No perceptible change, except now there's her realization of the superfluities of the questions that preoccupied her youth: if not a fussy housekeeper, nor an unconditionally devoted mother and wife, then what? If she wasn't any of these, what was she? To think she is sixty-nine and still unsure, still peeling at the layers of her self. The last eighteen years a waste.

She is capable of meanness. What else would you call the coldness she offered her husband after Eva's kiss? Although his torment was in plain sight for her to see. His conviction that she had seen through him, as if he reeked of that kiss. It wasn't clairvoyance but instinct that made her follow him to Eva's and Josephine's room that summer and watch them kiss, heard him making the young girl promise it would never happen again. She felt the stab of jealousy, her eyes prickling, her knees floundering with the sight of him reaching toward another, away from her.

She motions for her granddaughter to sit next to her. Marie gives her a hug and says, shyly, "You scared us, you know, going off in a blizzard! We'll have to keep a close eye on you from now on."

How young she is. Eva was only a couple years younger when she kissed Farid. Emilie traces her granddaughter's cheeks. As soft and fleshy as a plum. She has forgotten how radiant young skin is, as if life beats right below the surface. Perhaps it is the young who have got it right, with their impatient claims on life. Despite the long years behind her, she thinks one really has hardly any time at all.

She wasn't exactly angry at Eva. She and her niece had shared a passion for the same man. She had felt deeply embarrassed. She could not look Eva in the eye after that.

She wraps his bathrobe tightly around her chest and looks at him and smiles. She tells her family that his wife and son are dead. That his wife was an artist, and that he has given her several of her wooden statues to keep. She says it in an all-knowing tone, relishing the fact that she knows things they don't and the way they look at her now with a mixture of astonishment, interest, and new respect. She understands what it must have been like to be Farid, to have an audience so tantalized.

She looks at him again, motions at the bag of kafta, and utters one of the few words she knows in English: "Eat!" Whether to be polite or because he is really hungry, he reaches for the bag, and, with utter delight, she watches him bite into the meat. She knows she is not imagining his smile.

31

SALMA ISN'T SURE what they are doing in the house of this stranger. There's the hint of a smell she doesn't like. Yet it doesn't look that bad, she thinks, taking a look around, except for the dust on the bookshelves. Not many books on those shelves. In fact there's very little to get in the way of a good cleaning: a red couch in the middle where Emilie and Marie are now sitting, a dead plant in one of the corners, a couple of chairs by the fireplace, one occupied by Mr. Finch, or whatever his name is, who is now wiping his hands clean on a paper towel after eating some of Emilie's kafta, and the other chair by none other than herself. It makes her feel slightly extravagant, sitting across from him, feeling deliciously comfortable by the fire after their infernal walk through the blizzard. She wouldn't mind a little nap.

Never before has Salma felt as fearful for her life as during that walk from their house. Not even during the war. She doesn't know what happens when you stay out too long in the cold. She has heard several stories: how your ears fall off like dead leaves. How the body freezes first, before the heart has fully stopped. As a child, when she would make herself stop moving, she still felt the sun on her skin, her blood running in her veins. Freezing to death is an awful way to die. Parts snapping, plummeting to the frozen ground. She finds the stillness terrible, despite the wind that lifts and carries and wails. There's a fury and wrath about it she doesn't like. In the sun, things seem more innocuous and benevolent, furies impermanent.

It must have been this fear of freezing in the middle of their yard that made her walk faster than she ever had. In no time, she had caught up with her daughter, and the two of them trudging and breathing side by side instantly calmed her. They found George and Josephine in front of their neighbor's house. They were standing there without moving. It was she who broke the stillness. With a hand on her husband's shoulder she nudged him forward. "Go on," she said, and he brushed the snow off his face and walked over to the door.

This is a time of thawing, she thinks, sinking deeper into the chair. And this Mr. Finch, sitting across from her. She doesn't know what to say to him, except to thank him every once in a while for his hospitality. She has the distinct impression she bores him.

It is the oddest thing, Emilie leaving food and getting statues in return. Salma stiffens a little at the thought that it is with her food that Emilie has been making a show of generosity. Salma doesn't understand. What in the devil possessed her mother-in-law to take the first step and make contact with this man who, with never so much as a greeting or a smile in all the years he has lived here, has expressed any interest in reaching out like a normal neighbor?

Earlier she felt snubbed when Emilie made that remark about her excesses. Acknowledged, but snubbed. Emilie looked so self-satisfied as if she, Salma, were an old hat. As if no one fussed about germs anymore. What was that French word they used in Lebanon to describe a person who didn't keep up with the newest trends, who was stale and old-fashioned? *Démodée*. She, Salma, was *démodée* for striving to be a good housekeeper. The train has long left the station and she's been sitting on the bench all this time, scrubbing away at the stains.

There's definitely a smell here she can't identify. She stops short of sniffing the air, for this Mr. Finch is looking straight at her.

Oh, but look at Marie bending over to kiss her grandmother. What a lovely sight. She sighs contentedly (this fire is filling her with happiness). She feels part of a real family, for once. And there are Josephine and George standing by the couch, talking. What are they saying? She perks her ears but can't make it out. It's all right. She doesn't feel left out this once, doesn't fear that someone is trying to pull one over on her.

"This is a nice house," she tells him, just because she thinks she has to make conversation. Also, because George's and Josephine's hushed discussion on the other side is starting to irritate her.

"Where are you from?" he asks without acknowledging her compliment.

That's it, she thinks. He had to ask. She crosses her ankles, tightens her body into the chair that creaks from her weight and looks at him, her eyes narrowed, her chin pointed at him in defiance.

But when she tells him, all he does is nod and say that a colleague at his last job was from Lebanon.

"I worked with computers," he replies briefly when she asks what he does for a living, clearly indicating he will not say any more. Marie has a computer and it looks complicated, and this Mr. Finch, she concludes, must be an important man, although you wouldn't guess from looking at his house.

She scans the room and sees a picture of him with a woman and child on one of the shelves. The dead wife and son. She is curious but hesitates to ask. His tragedy (and still so young! He seems to be about her age. She doesn't think of herself as young, yet one is too young for some things) makes her shy around him. She knows what it's like to miss your family. Only last week she and George were talking about going back this summer for a visit. How they would take Emilie along. Sure, why not, she had laughed, shaking with excitement.

Pity stirs in her. No wonder his eyes are shifty and unsettled, as if he is constantly looking for the dead ones.

She is aware of him watching her, and she reddens and quickly turns away from the photograph.

"They died in strange circumstances," he says.

She is taken aback, already overwhelmed, for she can't really understand what he has said, but she makes herself look at him, silently willing him to go on.

"It was strange, the way they died," he repeats.

She looks at her family, mentally asking for their help, but they're not paying her any attention. George and Josephine are now talking by the window. Marie has her head on Emilie's lap. This man will tell her his story, and she will not understand a word of it.

Bravely, she leans forward, places a hand on his wrist, and asks him to speak slowly. He's singled her out to tell her this, and this allows her familiarities she would have never attempted before. In her request she means to convey urgency. She doesn't want to spoil her chances. On the other side of the fireplace, her husband and his sister are concocting God knows what, but she hardly gives them another thought. She wants to hear his story. She wants him to talk to her because, she realizes, this hasn't happened in a long time, this talking about anything beyond the store and Marie and what to make for lunch. She hasn't talked about anything important in a long time, and song, which, when she still had it, took the place of talk, has been lost to her.

She hears the names Myra (his wife?) and Brendan (his son?), and how Myra stopped to buy flowers on the side of the road and got out of the car, forgetting to put the brake on. How the car rolled back and crushed her while she tried to stop it, and the boy was thrown out and later died in the hospital from head injuries. "A stupid mistake," he continues, shaking his head. Myra was ordinarily so careful with their child. The only explanation he could find was the spring popping everywhere, making her unusually giddy that year, the fragrances intoxicating.

He hates flowers.

"Spring, it makes you happy," she says in a sudden burst of forwardness, "too happy," her fingers fluttering to her stomach. She got pregnant in spring.

While she held her breath under the cherry tree of her childhood, everything around her taunted her to let go. She tried resisting. Yet it happens whether you want it or not, this release. Always something on the inside pushing to get out. Like your water breaking. She wanted to hold on even then. She was terrified of childbirth. Had gotten used to that baby in her belly. One was always in the grip of something more powerful. She leaned over and touched his wrist.

She would like to console him. If George died, she would be devastated. He, George, would likely grieve for a long time if the reverse were true. The best of men, her husband, even if her heart isn't totally in it anymore.

He stokes the fire, a smile on his face, of regret perhaps for having opened up to this stranger?

Regret also, on her part, in the way she leans back in her chair, her natural reserve taking over again. Things stick to her. She warded off tragedy and death in Beirut and stayed beautiful. Yet here she succumbed. For eighteen years, life has been leaving on her face the mark of what she has seen. Has been filling her from the inside with stories she should have long forgotten. Here, in a peaceful town, life has been quietly catching up with her.

She starts talking. She can't stop herself. A child always leaves, she tells him and immediately regrets it. There are various kinds of leaving, his being the worst kind.

Her daughter asks her sometimes what language she dreams in. "Do you see me dreaming in English?" She chuckles.

"This might be just what I need," she says, still chuckling. First she'll start dreaming in English, next thing she'll be speaking the language like she was born to it. That's a thought. It would seep through to her brain, effortlessly, like water snaking through the dense earth. She saw it on that child specialist's show, how they play classical music to babies still in the womb. That Penelope woman with the thick glasses. Has he ever watched her show? No? She was very good. Salma learned a thing or two about child rearing that got her through some tough times! Bites her lip—too much talk about children. What's wrong with her? She wishes someone would reach through to the darkness of her brain and reorder those nooks and crannies in her head, because the way her brain is configured now, English doesn't fit.

She talks, spurred by the way he is looking at her.

"One time I really want to speak English," she says. Wished she spoke it like it was her birthright, with the precision of a blade, with the same copiousness as some of her best spreads, not the fragments she manages to muster.

"My heart still angry now. Ten years and I am still angry." She pounds her chest lightly to show him how hurtful the memory.

The day was bloated with the haze from the river and the rain that fell for three days in the heart of August and seemed to let up only to gather more power. On the fourth day, it finally stopped, so a trip to the park was in order to console Marie who'd been moping around the house all week with nothing to do. The grass was soggy and there were small pools of water on the benches. She wiped a dry spot to sit on and watch Marie play. In the park that morning were a young mother and her toddler who was more interested in the bark under his feet than in the playground equipment. There were also a couple of teenagers on the opposite bench. The boy's head was resting on the girl's lap and she caressed it like a child's.

Salma crossed her ankles and sat upright, pursing her lips, averting her eyes. "Young people in my country never do that. No touching. First you are married, then you can touch."

Marie was swinging. The toddler kept pushing bark in his mouth. The teenagers giggled. She rearranged the light sweater she had draped over her shoulders. The sky seemed to drop closer, as if swelling once again with rain.

It was the boy who said it. "You fucking spic, go back over the bridge." She still remembers the boy's words and repeats them quickly for their host's benefit, pausing to see his reaction. When he doesn't say anything, she continues.

Suddenly her daughter seemed distant and blurred, as if they were in two separate dreams. She knew enough English to understand the boy's words, to realize that some hostility had been released in the air around them. Her instinct was to duck and run for cover, but she was unable to move, and she felt her heaviness most acutely that day, as if her body had bulged on purpose over the years to anchor her on this bench and on that particular morning, under the dripping trees and the gray sky, and make her pay for some heinous sin. Slowly she made herself turn and look at the teenagers. They were talking and laughing as if nothing had been said, and for a moment she believed she had dreamed the incident. It wasn't the first time that her imagination had played tricks on her. She leaned forward on her bench and closed her eyes, and whispered to herself that yes, she must have surely imagined it all.

"Look, Mommy!" Marie shrieked, bending backward on the swing, her hair brushing the ground. Salma looked up at the sky and saw it with its dizzying hugeness. Then she heard them again, the despicable words, and she started falling, falling. She took another look around the park, hoping to find someone else for whom these words were intended. But the mother and her toddler had already left, and no one new emerged from the trees. She looked at them again, those lanky, scrawny kids she wouldn't have graced with a glance in her own country. But that was it: only a look, and no words to back it up, no means to tell them that filth is what she thought they amounted to. She dragged Marie home kicking and screaming, and she had George buy her a swing set so they would never have to return to that park.

"What's a spic, Mama?" Marie asked when they got home, tilting her head back and narrowing her eyes, the long look she gave her a rope tied around Salma's legs that held her to her spot.

"Nothing important," she said. "Now go."

And Marie did. But not before Salma heard the click of her child's mind's camera snapping, freezing her in that moment while she stood nervously wiping her hands on her apron, brushing away her hair, fidgeting.

She knew what a spic was. Some things you learn quickly. The pathologies of a country, its rifts and dishonesty. Across the bridge there was a community of Hispanics. Sometimes she went there to buy semolina before there was an aisle for international food in her local supermarket. She knew that she could protest all she wanted that she was not one of them, but there was also a name for people like herself. A name she didn't know but wished she did, because at least she might have blown it to smithereens. But what could she reply to being called a spic, except that she had the dark hair and complexion of another people, even more despised than the ones she had been mistaken for?

She grows silent. She doesn't tell him about the shame of these early years, how quickly she was put back in her place! Her Christian birth, which should have separated her from the Muslim Arabs and guaranteed her full admission to her new country, had not mattered. At the mall, the clerks asked her to repeat herself, and her manner of dress, conservative and fussy, looked foreign and attracted attention. To them, she was an Arab. At first, she made it a point to explain how much they shared: religion, dress, language (she would bring up French, which she still spoke better than she spoke English, although far from perfectly). But these explanations began to embarrass her. She was ashamed for them for imagining for a moment they might have been spared simply for the reason they had once been baptized.

She is not sure what he was able to make out of her rambling. He leans over and pats her hand. "They were stupid kids," he says. She knows he doesn't mean to be condescending, but she feels foolish for holding on to an old memory, for treating it all these years as if it held the key to her inexplicable sadness. Revealing it to him, who has lost wife and son and who is much more worthy of sympathy. Her cheeks burn. But the words are out, finally. Nothing to do now except let them linger as they may in this house to which she will probably never return, and leave her forever. She feels buoyed by the unburdening, and sheltered, from her memories and from the war that is taking place right now as they all sit in the calm of Mr. Finch's house. She takes in the moment, trying not to let her anxiety detract her from the pleasure she feels, and knowing full well that life will take notice sooner or later and turn her luck around, the way a fall or the wind flips a helpless bug over on its back.

Shame makes george garrulous. A voice in his head tells him their host must think them people of low breeding, incapable of keeping their house in order. And so the words pour out to divert his thoughts.

None of the others seem affected by these scruples. His wife looks quite the social butterfly, entertaining their host with a tale whose content he (his sister, too, he can see it plainly on her face) would give his right arm to know. He thinks he sees her batting her eyelashes although he can't be sure, with his glasses forgotten in the rush on the coffee table. And now here she is, patting their host on the wrist, such familiarity he has not seen her display before. It gives him great displeasure. To Josephine, he expresses the inappropriateness of finding themselves imposing on a stranger, and insists that they should take the first opportunity to leave. His sister gets mad at him. Undoubtedly, she is feeling left out, and he feels a surge of compassion for her. He dearly hopes that some good might come out of all this. Yet the possibility of a happy ending does not wipe out the humiliation of their present position. His mother who, by all accounts, of her age and her stature in the family, should have known better than to behave like an irresponsible child, has deeply embarrassed them, and yet his wife and sister are behaving as if they'd been invited to a dinner party, while his daughter, affecting her usual surliness, is barely acting politely.

He talks himself into finding the silver lining as he makes his way to the other corner of the house, miffed with the female bloc of his family where he finds himself outnumbered as usual and unheard.

If they were to stay the night and part of tomorrow, should the storm begin to peter out in the afternoon hours, Eva might show up and, not finding them at home, she'd have no choice but to return to New York. No, he corrects himself. She'd find a place in town and call the police. This would delay the moment when he'd have to meet her and would give him some time to compose a face for the occasion. He'd been avoiding the thought ever since he has learned of her visit, but he realizes now that he must face the inevitable. It was a long time ago. Water under the bridge. He has other fish to fry. He calculates: because of the snow, two days, perhaps three, deducted from seventeen days, the length of her stay. If you consider that he would be spending most of that remaining time between the store and his bed, the duration of time in her presence might not exceed a cumulative total of four days.

Warmed up by these calculations, his mind turns to the store where the ledger he keeps by hand is imprinted in his memory. With the price of milk and eggs going up, it will not be possible to keep the same decent margin of profit, but he might be able to make up for it by raising the price of his sandwiches twenty cents across the board. Despite the fuss he made earlier at home, their loss will not be that bad. A few egg sandwiches he'll have to throw out, which is a loss in sales, not small by any means, but if they tighten their belts for a week or two they'll pull through, provided they don't have many repeats of this storm. The tough winters are one of the few drawbacks of being in this part of the world. But, as they say about New England, if you don't like the weather, wait a minute. He'd found the saying very funny at first. Since then it has lost some of its freshness, yet he still prefers it to the other saying some of his customers insist on pronouncing with visible self-satisfaction the moment they set foot in his store on a rainy day. "This weather is for the ducks" has become one of his least favorites, but he forces himself to smile when he hears it, usually responding with a short "Pretty soggy, eh?" before returning to what he was doing.

Despite these snags (so small, really), he likes being at the store and he's happy with what he's accomplished there. A desire to let their host know he is more than this baffled head of family who can't keep his brood in check overtook him earlier. He might have talked a bit too much, as he knows he has the tendency to do when he's nervous, giving this Mr. Finch detailed directions to the store, plus the layout, which must not have been of great interest to his interlocutor who seemed a little bored with the explanations. You must have surely come in for a coffee or a loaf of bread at one point, he kept asking, to which his host had replied in the negative at first, then, probably weary, had changed to a noncommittal maybe. George boasted about the videos, how he liked to watch them from time to time. His favorites were the Rambo series, the only reason being—but this he omitted to tell his host—that Sylvester Stallone was one of the few American actors he was familiar with from his movie-watching days in Lebanon. Finally, he had the sense to switch the conversation away from himself and asked Mr. Finch what he did for a living. Rather surprisingly, Mr. Finch answered in the past tense. George didn't press for explanations. Discreetly, he took a look around. For someone who didn't seem to be holding a job, their host was not doing too badly. Stocks, undoubtedly. Maybe an unexpected inheritance. He wondered whether they would have to start seeing him from now on. The need to return the favor gnawed at him. He hated being in debt. Not one credit card to his name, although the store was franchised on credit, but what can you do, this is America. He extracted the promise from their neighbor that he would come over for dinner. In his mind, he was already planning the feast he would ask Salma to put together. He might even take them all to dinner at an Italian restaurant to impress him. He would send him a gift card from the store.

George wonders if he should worry about his mother, yet she seems in a good enough mood, not at all repentant. He will have to make sure this never happens again. He tries joking with Marie but she responds with a straight face. He must admit that "Fancy meeting you here!" is not one of his most amusing lines, but it's all he can think of to lighten the mood. Yet he is hurt by his daughter's rejection. He can typically count on her to take his side. He feels like a child, moping around, waiting for someone to pay attention to him. The feeling humiliates him enough to make him take action. Years of discipline, when anxiety has pushed him to verbal excesses that wore down on his listeners, has taught him this. He takes a deep breath and sees before his eyes numbers neatly stacked in his favor, shelves emptied and replenished daily, walls freshly painted, the humming of the refrigerators like background music, and the cascade of the soda bottles in their chutes snatched by eager hands a tribute to his foresight and a balm to his aching, thwarted heart.

"FOR THE FOURTH TIME, I don't know when we will go home," Josephine snaps.

Her brother is worried about the bad impression they must be making. People of tact and good upbringing they are, who would never dream of invading a man's privacy. "It's totally out of character for her to take off like that," George underlines within earshot of their neighbor. How astonishing, she thinks, their mother taking off in the middle of a blizzard and causing an upheaval. Yet Loom doesn't look put out, not in the least, despite what her nag of a brother thinks. A decent host, offering hot chocolate and shelter, and, although not effusively, clearly happy with the kafta. Buddying it up with Salma by the fire, her sister-in-law looking flushed and ridiculously giddy. And while not exactly chatty, he is well-mannered, graceful even in his reserve, which she sees as the outward manifestation of a tolerant soul, affably taking in their commotion in their moment of crisis without the least shock or judgment.

"Stop fussing," she whispers and rolls her eyes when her brother walks away in a huff. The snow is still falling heavily. She can't see how they have any choice but to stay put.

She sits on the rug next to Marie who's flipping through magazines. Josephine twirls the rug's fringes. She likes being here, in this house with the man she still prefers to call Loom. The two of them haven't exchanged more than a few words. Her mother and her sister-in-law have been luckier. Josephine would give her right hand to know what Salma is telling him right now in a soft voice and why he reaches over to pat her hand. Josephine looks at her mother who is sitting on the sofa as quiet as can be.

Perhaps, like Josephine, she is feeling jealous. Why else would she suddenly bolt to her feet and announce her wish to cook?

"Mother, I am sure Mr. Finch would rather you didn't," Josephine says quickly, while George seconds her words with energetic nods, clearly in a panic.

But their mother will hear none of it. Sheepishly, they translate her wishes to Loom who throws his arms in the air, which Josephine interprets as a sign that they have worn out their welcome, until he explains that he doesn't keep much food in the house. But upon seeing Emilie's disappointment, he disappears into the basement to return with a packet of meat he lays on the coffee table, a roast beef purple with freezer burn that puts a big smile on Emilie's face.

She follows her mother and their host into the kitchen. Loom produces a bag of onion and garlic gone to sprout, which her mother, salvaging what she can, chops and leaves in a pan to soften with olive oil while the roast beef thaws in the microwave. Josephine hears Salma and George come up behind her. Together they must seem like clingy children. And the same way she would difficult children, Emilie orders them out. Bravely, they linger, and she commands them again, this time with a tone that suffers no contradiction.

Josephine goes back to sit next to Marie who is now sprawled close to the fire, hands held out to the flames. She is badly craving a cigarette. As far as she can tell, Loom doesn't smoke, yet she gets up and walks over to the bookshelves and rummages among the few books, craning her neck to try to make out what is going on behind the kitchen door. She hears the clanging of pots and water running and voices talking softly. She yawns and digs vainly in her pockets in search of a stray cigarette, then goes to sit near Salma. There is no easy way to ask her sister-in-law what she and Loom were talking about before her mother interrupted them. Nothing in the two women's history that would make it possible to ask and come out unrebuked.

She knows nothing. The realization makes her hunch into herself. She eats and showers and goes to work and spies on Loom, and knows nothing. She is as raw and inexperienced as the day she came here more than eighteen years ago, briefly alive with a sexual affair conducted under a lemon tree. Fleeing a war and the power of a cousin she adored. Barely holding on, mustering enough life skills to get by, unmussed.

Eva. If they stay here Eva will not be able to find them. The thought lifts her spirit. Let her worry for a change, let her scramble and search and wonder if she will ever see their faces again, and find out what it feels like to be stranded alone in a world she has no inkling how it works. Let Eva be alone in a foreign land and flounder through the knee-deep snow and the miserable, cold world. Let her knock and receive no answer. Josephine almost pants with the satisfaction. Salma is looking at her curiously.

"I think we should check on Mother and Mr. Finch," she says, rising from her chair.

34

IF SHE HAS STAKED HER CLAIM, Emilie is not apologetic. She has gone out of her way to find him. Snuck out like a teenager to bring him food. Trampled a lettuce patch once. And today she has gone in the teeth of the storm and found him. He does not remind her of anyone she knows, with his blue eyes and day-old beard, his half-hearted concessions to conversation, and the way he keeps to himself then smiles unexpectedly and lets on that he has been waiting to be found. Yet for all his foreignness, she feels she can talk to him, this grieving man who is half her age and whose language she doesn't understand. She can tell him how all of a sudden she panicked. About Yussef, and her niece who is on her way. Fled toward him, he who was in need of food. And he would tell her how right she had been to come.

She works quickly, David carrying out her orders, opening cupboards too high for her to reach, washing the canned beets and the corn and greens beans she has found in the pantry. Luckily he has rice and she washes two cups in the sink until the water runs clear. She sets the rice on the stove to cook while the roast browns with the onion and the garlic. Finally, she covers the meat with water and crumbles in a bouillon cube, and gives it a quick stir before sitting down.

They sit across the table from each other, the bowl of canned vegetables between them. She has no idea what to do with them, but she will find something. She is full of confidence. Casually, her finger traces circles on the table. The silence between them peaceful, comfortable, as if they've said all the words that needed saying and are now basking in the afterglow of a good, solid connection. David pops a few kernels of corn in his mouth.

"Tawlah," she says. He looks at her quizzically then gets her drift. He repeats the word and says, "Table." "Koursi," she says next and he repeats it and gives her the translation. "Chair." It is her turn to repeat after him. Their exchange stays limited to the extent of their common experience: cooking, household furniture, everyday objects. In his eyes, she sees the ghosts of his wife and son. What does he see in hers? For she presumes that she also carries her losses in her eyes. Their sorrow in plain sight. And yet they talk about spoons and green beans, and laugh at their disastrous pronunciation. Clearly it is enough. Clearly they need not say more.

They continue in this fashion, until the rest walk in on them and find them with a heap of sodden vegetables on the table between them, and the delicious smell of cooking wrested miraculously from a dubious piece of meat and stale roots slowly filling the kitchen.

PRETTY SOON the rest of the crowd, with the exception of the young girl, has joined them in the kitchen. What of that! David tells Myra silently. Can't stretch my hospitality much beyond this point, I'm afraid, my dear.

The man, George, is telling him again about his store downtown, and yes, David says wearily, he's sure he's been there a couple of times. George's wife tastes the green beans when the old woman isn't looking, and his sister blushes every time David looks in her direction.

"We can't thank you enough. We will leave as soon as possible," the man is saying. David assures him they can stay as long as is needed.

I hope you're happy, hospitable woman. I've never been much for small talk, and I won't be starting today. But the smells are so good, my Myra. I haven't had real food in a long time.

David loiters in the kitchen, opens the refrigerator and looks inside. He is not sure what they want from him. If only he could figure it out, a great burden would be lifted from him. He looks anxiously at the window and remembers how, weeks after Myra's and Brendan's deaths, he began feeling like a man with a fatal illness, free in his remaining time on earth to spend his time as he saw fit. Grief unbound him. He gave up job and friends and left New York for the wilderness of Vermont. But for the grace of God, he repeated to himself, although he was still not religious. But the words reminded him to renounce what was not essential. And now, in this same spirit, he discards his good manners and say to his uninvited guests, "I must leave."

They lurch towards him and he extends his hand to keep them away, palms pressing against the greedy earnest air, his eyes darting anxiously at the window. The mound is still standing where he left it, the top uneven. He will tamp it down and hollow out an entrance. When it's all finished, he will paint it in stripes of pink, blue, orange and green, like the clay duck Brendan made in art class. Wavy stripes as if the duck carried the water in its feathers. Its tail a bowl for loose change, the stripes there crisscrossed. An orange stripe encircles the body all the way up to the pink bill and the blue crest, like a rope pulling it forward. The name of his boy carved in capital letters in the white bottom before it hardened, the tail of the "a" a tiny knob of dried clay.

He runs outside. The icy air is welcome after the stifling heat of the house. His muscles are aching for movement. He picks up the shovel and starts hacking away at the bumps. I am not ready for this yet. His movements are bigger than they need to be. He suspects their eyes on him. He digs the blade in, sending shards of snow flying. He finds out that he can press against the shaft of the shovel with his stomach and raze through like a human bulldozer.

He works for more than an hour at this pace, leaving deep gouges. His speed is hampered by the snow on the ground and he realizes that he's going about it the wrong way. It will take him days to achieve the smoothness he desires. He throws the shovel away, takes a few deep breaths, and stands back to assess the situation. The paint will cover some of the bumps. What he needs are achievable goals, a strategy of pinpointing at the most blatant defects and removing them. A stratagem, a girdling of the bulges with strokes of paint. Ruse and illusion the cornerstones of art. And yet. Think of the resolve of the duck, the naïve whiteness of its underbelly, the lines wavering, like cloth flapping in the wind. How it touched him when he saw it, with its cupped tail and exuberant plumage. He asked Brendan if he could have it to keep on his desk where it has stayed ever since, pointing sweetly toward a world it alone can see.

He sits in the snow. He doesn't know how to finish the igloo. His house is full of strangers who ask something of him he cannot give. An old woman is cooking him food. For the first time in a year, he has talked to other human beings besides store clerks or gas attendants. The snow covers him and he sinks slowly under a spinning white wall, which both weighs him down and alights on him like an embrace.

IN THE KITCHEN, Josephine hears the familiar noises of cooking, although the makeup of the cooking team is startling. Her mother and Salma, sleeves pulled, come to an agreement about the fate of the canned vegetables, which would benefit, it is decided, from a thorough sautéing in olive oil and the addition of extra flavorings. Salma shakes the pan and sprinkles spices and herbs. Emilie picks up the roast with a fork and turns it to cook on the other side. "What do you think? Enough salt? Should I turn the heat to low?" They taste, ponder, add this or that. They chop vegetables, open drawers that do not belong to them and spice up the food to their liking as if they have been doing this all their lives, together in a stranger's kitchen, moving about with the efficiency of experienced collaborators.

Despite their limited English, they got through to him. Perhaps not a small accomplishment, to have a man sit facing you with genuine interest in his eyes. To have him lean over, help you out when you fumbled with words, his eyes never leaving your face. She wouldn't know. Her own eyes were busy wandering. From his hair, revealed, finally, hatless: a dark brown with streaks of gray. His face, which she finds pleasing: the features mild and proportionate, a few years younger than hers; the small blue eyes sitting on either side of a slim nose; the lips slightly fleshy, the impression agreeably, comfortingly ordinary; a face she might have seen a thousand times before. Down to his hands, small and rough from working outside.

She wants to ask him about that. About the mound he has accumulated in the front. Like a beacon to safety, she wants to tell him, guiding the stray. How did they manage to see it in the blizzard? All of it white, and yet its height and bumps creating shadows that even in the gray light they spotted. She wants to thank him effusively for it, feels her heart warm up with gratitude. She will not tell him about watching him from her room, nor will she say anything about her boring life. She might talk about the mountains of Lebanon and the jasmine and gardenia in their garden, and about the war that destroyed their world. After that, nothing. She will only say that, and not go into the details of the boredom and futility of the last eighteen years.

She has had two cups of chocolate. If she is caught, it will be her excuse. Intoxicated on chocolate. On words roiling dangerously in her head. On her anger at having been denied the chance once again of seeing a man lean over to better hear her. Her feet giddy and irresponsible, taking her to the stairs in the hallway and up to where the bedrooms must be. A door ajar, she opens and enters. The curtains drawn, the shadow of a large desk, a chair in the corner. When she flicks the switch, she sees an array of papier-mâché masks and statuettes of shepherds and dogs, bells in different sizes, clay snakes and baskets, insignias with unusual carvings, the whole painted in bright, vibrant colors. "Wondrous!" she says out loud, her arms extended, speaking to an invisible audience. Her Loom. The man she has watched all these months, rapt by his mystery. She touches the creations on the desk one by one, lightly, a bit unsteady on her feet. Look at all this, Eva. A man of genius, my Loom.

The possessive is her right. Loom is her creation. She will not call him David yet. She takes the smallest of the bells, painted gold, and puts it in her palm. The clay must have been rubbed with very fine sandpaper to achieve the smoothness of metal. For the first time, she understands that the flared bottom might have been designed with more than an aesthetic purpose, back when church bells served as community broadcasters. Its function must have been to diffuse sound through the land, sending it in perfect concentric echoes to every corner of the community.

The circle is the perfect shape, she decides, walking to a small table by the window. The sun heats up the entire earth. Not all at once, but a big chunk of it all the same. Imagine the stingy output of an angular source. She pretends to shudder at the thought. The planets themselves are round, fated into their optimal shape by bulk and gravity.

She must have known he would have a picture of his son and wife in every room. It is so very sad, she murmurs, taking in her hands the picture of the lovely boy and the woman beaming at the camera. To her, right now, he is David, the man behind the camera, who must have had an inkling, when taking this photo, of the wisdom of capturing what he could. It is very sad, she repeats, and places the picture back on the table.

She hears him come in and turns around. At first he looks surprised to find her here, then irritated, although he is too polite to chastise her openly. His face is red from the cold and his eyes puffy, as if he has been crying.

"I have been watching you," she blurts out before losing her nerve. "I like the color you painted the house. The shed is coming out nicely. Perhaps you need a new car, you've been working on this a long time and God knows it's not going any faster."

She chuckles and pushes a lock of hair away from her face. "These are beautiful," she says, pointing at the desk. "You're really good with your hands."

"I have been watching you," she adds and looks away, waiting for him to say something.

She knows it isn't wise to pause, to give him a chance to push her out. She catches herself calling him Loom and stops. Loom he isn't. He is David, a man she will probably never really know, a neighbor who took them in kindly and must by now be waiting patiently for them to leave. Despite her loneliness, she knows that the distance separating them cannot be crossed with words, that it takes more than opening up candidly to be heard. For the last eighteen years, she has been talking to ghosts. She is out of practice.

His eyes are not unkind but they are clearly bidding her to go.

"It is something I have learned to do," he says. "I was never the artist before."

She knows this is not the beginning of a conversation. For a reason she doesn't know, he continues to be courteous despite her intrusion.

"You are very good," she adds, preferring to ignore the hint, staying.

"This is a private room," he says more directly. His eyes sad but firm. She has asked for it.

"Then I must leave." Her voice shaking a little. Coming out of a dream and into the harsh light. She gets some of her composure back. Fool, crazy fool.

"I am sorry." He takes her by the arm and leads her to the door. "I will be down in a minute."

The door closes behind her. And the kindness of strangers does not lighten the load of a life unlived.

37

She must tell him. Before they leave and maybe never see each other again, for being neighbors is no guarantee that they will. How kind his gifts. How she could tell the figurines apart with her eyes closed, her finger her guide. How she saw him in her mind's eye, brows knotted, bent over, his eyes intently watching the shape as it sprung to life between his hands. Even now, when she knows it was his wife who had carved them, she holds on to the thought. The eggs she kept in her pocket, sometimes a few at a time, reminding her every time she touched them that there was something beyond this, this house in the middle of nowhere with children who had stopped talking; something salvageable still. She had been right all along: human connection held them sanely together, like the string that had once held Shirin's rosary together. For each movement of the finger, a bead stands briefly alone, heaved by prayer. Break the rosary, as Eva once did, and we are lost, scattered to the winds. As she herself had done, when she accused Yussef and sent him to the asylum to die among strangers.

Each statue a story. The boy with the untucked shirt perhaps David himself as a child, impatient and unkempt, racing out to play. The girl squatting with her right hand extended to pluck a flower or caress a stray dog must have haunted his dreams with her beseeching eyes. Cupid with his round belly and dimpled knees. Shepherds with tattered clothes that David must have seen in children's books, because she has yet to see a shepherd in Scarabee. Children with the placid faces of beings who keep too much to themselves. And there were the eggs. Holding them in her hand she could almost sense a beat, feel them almost opening. Of all the creations he gave her they are the most difficult to understand, the most hidden and closed.

She casts a last look around her. Salma, the kitchen scoured clean and the dishes washed and dried, is all smiles and jolly busyness. Emilie would have never managed this on her own. Would have left the kitchen a sorry mess, dirty pots and pans strewn like the dead in the wake of a battle.

"The kitchen looks great," she says.

Salma smiles in return. Emilie must remember to be more mindful. Kindness is harder to carry out than most people think.

Another half an hour and the meat will be falling off the bones.

In the living room, her son and her granddaughter are watching TV. She strokes Marie's lovely red hair and stops to laugh at the juggler performing for a cheering audience. She folds the blanket she used earlier and leaves it on the arm of the sofa. George looks up and asks where she is heading. She puts a finger on her lips and he doesn't insist, happy to return to the juggler. He laughs, his belly shaking. She grabs the figurines from her bag, all seventeen of them, and puts them with the eggs in her pockets. Josephine is staring out the window. She stands next to her. "Tomorrow it will be over," she tells her. How she has neglected her daughter. "When Eva comes, we will show her a good time." Her daughter's shoulders stoop. How will she help her?

She walks up to his room and lays the content of her pockets on the desk. When she begins to talk, he stares at her. She prefers to look away because she is afraid he might become bored with the words she is saying, the Arabic he doesn't understand.

She tries to explain why she came to him in the middle of a blizzard, why he had been leaving her his wife's art. She thinks the two of them were waiting to be found.

She is returning his gifts, she says, because they are what remain of his wife. She doesn't think it was an accident, his leaving them to her by the clearing. She thinks his wife is looking after him. After her, too, perhaps, she says more quietly, afraid she has gone too far. "But," she raises her head and looks frankly at him, "when you leave your home you break a trail. Do you understand? Boundaries become less . . ." she waves her hand in the air, "solid." There's this wavering feeling for a long time, and the notion that anything is possible might be the only hard truth. And so, the idea that his wife has brought them together doesn't seem as absurd as that.

She is so very thankful, more than he will ever know. He is a good man and she would be proud to count him as her friend.

He looks at her, his eyes entirely without curiosity but not unkind. When she is finished, she stands up from her chair and gives him a smile before leaving the room. She's not sure she's said all she wanted to say or even if all of it was true, but she is convinced that, although she will never be completely free of her past, the parts that she regrets the most have loosened their hold on her in this room whose door she now gently closes behind her.

THE SUN SLANTING FROM THE WINDOW falls on the counter scrubbed clean. The dishes have been put away, the sheets laundered, and the beds made before their departure. Earlier, he had heard them busying themselves and had stayed in bed, enjoying the noises of a house being put in order.

The only trace left of them is a slight whiff of fried onion. The silence has returned, but it is a different kind of silence than the one he's been accustomed to the last two years. An interlude rather than a constant, their recent presence still echoing and yielding, despite their efforts to leave no trace of their visit, enough material clues (the blankets folded rather than tossed in closets, the kitchen towel where he would have never left it, hanging from the oven's door, the perfect spotlessness he would have never achieved himself, with his tendency to ignore certain facets of disarray) to remind him how faded his earlier memories seem in comparison, despite his best efforts.

To his surprise, he'd been able in the end to produce from his kitchen the makings of a decent meal. He'd found food in the cupboards he had forgotten existed. His tongue, too, had loosened in conversation at the dinner table, his mind recalling information from before Vermont, when he was still well read and his photographic memory filed every bit of knowledge away for potential use. Information so precise they were amazed and, it seemed to him, grateful, that he knew so much about their country and its struggles.

After dinner, he sat next to Josephine and talked to her about what she had seen in the room upstairs. How all of a sudden, after the death of his wife and child, he was overtaken by the urgent need to use his hands to create beauty. He felt them near him when he worked (Myra had been an artist, and Brendan had shown great promise), their fingers twined through his. He himself would never be good. They could go back to the room if she wished (but she didn't) and he would show her how imperfect his creations really were. But they were a great improvement on what he had been able to achieve before. A klutz if he had ever seen one, totally hopeless with his hands. And yet, he'd managed a few things with plaster and papier-mâché thanks to the library, which housed some excellent books on arts and crafts.

Yes, he was always tinkering, fixing broken things, he acknowledged to one of her remarks. As for the mound he was building outside, it was something he had meant to do for a long time and that would be completed in due time. At any rate, it wasn't something he wished to dwell on right now. But, he added, aware that he had slighted her once and was now taking great pains to wipe out his rudeness, she would soon be able to see it from her window and tell him what she thought. He saw her blush at being caught watching him from her window and, to level things out, he complimented her on the garden, which he said he had admired every summer since he moved here. At which she looked visibly relieved and, encouraged by his loquaciousness, she told him how much joy the garden gave her. Every time she bit into a tomato or smelled a sprig of mint, she was transported to a happier place. If she could have one wish, it would be for a life of perpetual summer.

He listened carefully to her every word. While working on the igloo before dinner (fruitlessly—he had felt suddenly so angry with their presence, so afraid they had come to rob him of something that he had dashed outside and smashed at the mound), he thought he knew why they were in his home. For a while he imagined that all he had to do was sit back and let them take what they needed. For he had felt, ever since they had set foot in his house, perhaps even before, when Emilie had started bringing him food, that something was required of him. He had accepted this, balking occasionally (he had stopped leaving Myra's statues), but, generally, he had made peace with the inescapable fact of their presence. And then he had gone in and found Josephine in the room upstairs and had acted rudely.

After he had practically kicked her out, and although he could tell that she had not disturbed anything, he had rearranged everything, moving the big bell a little more to the center, spreading out the turtles and the ducks. Then he had sat in the chair and closed his eyes, perhaps dozing off for a few moments, because the scene he recollected next was as vivid as the dreams he had right after the accident, his yearning so strong it brought Myra and Brendan back to life the minute he closed his eyes.

This time, it was Myra alone he saw. Standing in the doorway, while he fussed with his tie and inhaled a granola bar. Her arms folded against her chest, leaning with her right shoulder against the frame. A dress he had not seen before, and yet it did not look new, sleeveless and with lace around the collar. He could see the silhouette of her legs against the light and was aroused. He could have stayed and made love to her. His meeting wasn't for another hour. But there were vases of flowers on every table. He thought that he saw her snickering and was aware that he was running away as he grabbed his attaché and banged the door behind him, stifling the sneeze that threatened to explode from his nasal passages until he was safely swallowed by the elevator.

"I'm sorry," he muttered, opening his eyes. The tears could still flood him in an instant, the pain still feel raw as the first day.

Everyone had expressed their sorrow to him, and he had found that, although it did not bring back Myra and Brendan, it was comforting nevertheless. They wished things had been different. They would change what had happened, if only they could.

For the thousandth time, he imagined it, the Mercedes, suddenly unrestrained, a wild, unstoppable beast. Myra, his strong Myra who had hauled him up the mountain with a rope tied around their waists, trying to stop the hulking metal with her body, to roll it back up the hill. How much courage it must have taken her, to know that she stood no chance, but to try anyway to slow down its descent because Brendan was panicking in the back seat, and because she knew, even though she had called on him to stay put, that he had unbuckled his seat belt the moment she had stopped on the side of the road to buy flowers. But the car continued its course and barely slowed when it passed over Myra's body, gaining speed from the frenzied spinning of its wheels, the tilt of the hill, and didn't stop until it hit an old maple tree that crumpled it to a fraction of its former size and ejected his only son from the window left open for the breeze to enter. It was small consolation for David to know that his son had not smashed through the glass, that his flight for a few short seconds had been as smooth and light as a bird's. He alighted on the tree's protruding roots, his wounds all internal. As for Myra, she bore on her arms and chest the silt of the wheels, the bruises and slashes of her lost struggle.

It happened very fast, the eyewitness said, a woman in her forties, breathless with the scope of what she had seen. "I am so sorry."

"You won't even look at me!" Myra had followed him to the elevator that same morning while he fled to let out the sneeze he could no longer stifle and drain the congestion that made every square inch of his face ache. Like a schoolboy unsure of the right answer, he had avoided her eyes every time she confronted him. To force him to look, she had started leaving lists in strategic spots. When he went to open the refrigerator door or brush his teeth, he had to stare at the parent conference she'd had that day, the dinner pot luck she would shop for the next morning, all the volunteering she was doing at their son's school. Indictment glared at him from every corner. The more she hounded him the more unresponsive he became, his stupid stubbornness kicking in. He knew he wasn't doing enough, yet he dug in his heels, and fled every chance he got to his office in the city and his own computer consulting company that he had started in his twenties and had grown to fifteen employees he directed with a strong hand. He fled from the wood shavings she never swept and the full sink and the unmade beds (she had fired the housekeeper), and most of all he fled from her disappointment. And even though she never said it, he suspected that sometimes she wished she had stuck to her initial answer when he had proposed that first time.

He spent Saturdays with his son. Sometimes she came along, to fairs and bike rides and trips to the ice cream stand, and they had a great time, his guard down, her misgivings forgotten, the pleasure of being together reddening their cheeks. Sometimes she stayed home to catch up on her alone time, as she put it, and that, too, was fine. She had not planned on having a child so soon, and it had been difficult for her to quit her job at the dance school and do her sculpting on a part-time basis. He knew he could have given her back the things she missed by being home more often. He was his own boss, she reminded him, the sarcasm not lost on him. But the idea of leaving someone else in charge appalled him. And so he continued in his course, knowing that he was only deferring trouble.

When she started filling the house with flowers, he knew they had reached that point. She'd been shocked to find out about his allergies the first year they went out together, the violence of the migraines that seized him around pollen, his battered sinuses knocking him out for days. Still, he would not give in. He was angry at her attempt to rouse him, to force him to respond. All she had accomplished, he told himself, was to make him feel righteous whenever he spent less time at home.

He could bring up his mother's despotism, wrest out some justification for his easily injured pride that made benign requests seem like orders he refused to carry out. Yet all this would serve to do would be to elucidate without exempting, and maybe not even that. Maybe the true explanation lay in his own inventiveness, his ability to imagine himself easily aggrieved, in his need to break away again and again from the helplessness of childhood.

He looks out the window and sees them walking away. There is no telling if he has given them what they need, although he can say that he tried. For the first time in his life, he has not run away when something was asked of him. Yet there is no telling if he has come anywhere near succeeding.

He goes out and kneels down to enter the igloo. His head grazes the ceiling. If he extends his arms, he can touch the walls. He has spent hours carving the interior, smoothing down any bumps until the effect is that of a perfect circle, a wave cresting and falling back upon itself. Yet he feels contained, anchored to the ground beneath him. He thinks of baby Moses tossed upon the Nile in his cradle of bulrushes, making it to safe anchor and to the arms of the pharaoh's daughter whose heart had been aching for the infant boy. Providence smiled on her that day. Perhaps she had willed him to emerge from the water, glittering and unscathed like a merboy, and take his place among her people. But maybe he was the one who had found his way to her, steering through the strong river with his sleepy eyes, his heart trustingly beating inside the basket lovingly woven by his mother who had had to entrust him to the water in order to save him from the evil pharaoh.

All along he had held on to this secret hope. The crazy, unwarranted hope that he would make it to shore. He looks for signs that he is there.

Self-betterment, driven into him as a boy, remains his gauge. Has he not only a few minutes ago compared himself to an infant, coming to the realization finally that control, once so dear, might have always eluded him? With their deaths, he was set adrift, as blind and defenseless as a newborn. Has he not left behind all that he had known, his business and the state where he lived all his life to come to this new land, in its way as unfamiliar as a new country? Surely such shifts in his soul must presage the rumblings of a new beginning. He hoped he would be rescued, hauled up the mountain again.

The daylight streams through the arched entrance of the igloo, and yet he has brought an oil lamp, not to light his way but as a way of inaugurating it. He has read that in melting and refreezing, the igloo is greatly strengthened. A real igloo stands a greater chance of survival, all the living done within it coiling to bolster the walls. His igloo will disintegrate quickly, with a single oil lamp and its solitary flame licking at the glass and exuding inadequate heat. Despite its short life expectancy, lasting the duration of a season that itself is nearing its end, he wants his igloo to be solid. He focuses his gaze in the hope he might see a sign, something to tell him he is not alone. To get a glimpse of you is why I have built this. A promise fulfilled, a shelter of snow. The thing by which you can perish saving you.

He is warmed by the lamp. He thinks he sees beads of moisture on the wall, as if the igloo is sweating. Your wife has been looking after you, he thinks he understood Emilie saying. You are doing a great job, Daddy. He is not worthy, and yet good fortune keeps coming his way. Memories tumble like ripe fruit into his lap. He can hear the lisp in Brendan's speech, Myra's sudden intakes of breath before the first cut to a piece of wood; their individual cadences, the way they favored particular words and patterns; he can hear their pauses and the way their silence fell upon his discerning ears to register either great happiness or great disappointment. All the things he ignored or skirted before, he now hears with the boundless limpidness of the white that surrounds him. Brendan and Myra. Myra and Brendan. If they appear before him, he will fill his eyes while he can.

The wind returns, audible. This is his only chance, kneeling down in this shell carved out of the bones of winter, his house a small distance away. Moses' journey across the Nile was short, spotted by his sister who, squinting in the distance, saw him being pulled out of the water and into the princess's lap, and look at how his life turned out. David waits. If they appeared, would he recognize them? But that fear, too, is quickly dissipated in the certainty that the past remains, even when, transformed and almost unrecognizable, it is scattered, over and over across the beach, like the great wreck of a ship slowly melting into the swelling waves.

39

THE PLANE TRIP from New York to Boston is short enough for Eva to feel as though she has barely left land. She tosses a bag of peanuts in the air and catches it, which seems to annoy the passenger on her left, a middle-aged woman with bleached hair who keeps shifting in her seat and sighing in exasperation. The plane is full of crabby people who, like her, were grounded by the storm. At least she has a window seat. She turns her back to them and looks out at the sky, which is now a beautiful blue with lovely puffs of clouds hovering about the wings of the plane.

The holidays. They were her pretext for picking up the phone to say she was coming, as if without this excuse they might have found a way to dissuade her. Her bags full of goodies, although who knows if her gifts will be enough to deter from the scrutiny they will subject her to upon arrival, weighing in advance the extent of the disturbance her visit will wreak.

Books and sweets, she is bringing, women's magazines and CDs, and nuts from her aunt's favorite roastery. Photographs, also, some that will sadden them, the line of trees in front of their old apartment cut to widen the road, and, here and there, despite their best efforts to wipe that chapter of their past out of the streets, lingering signs of the war, buildings still riddled with bullet holes, refugees squatting in deserted apartments, their rags drying on the lines. Other photos will cause them to cry out in delight. For this is a Beirut they will not recognize, restaurants and coffee shops spilling out their tables and chairs on sidewalks jammed with people out for a good time, and an ancient city thousands of years old discovered and dug up from the ruin, absolving, with the weight of its age and the gripping tale of its long burial, the staggering disorder. A lively and riotous city her aunt Emilie might recognize. When the war started, Eva and her cousins were too young to know anything except their own tight quarters in the Christian section. They will be dazzled and might envy her this belated acquaintance with a city now spectacularly returned to life.

She would have liked to carry in her luggage other things as well, a pinch of soil, a recording of the sea and perhaps, charitably, of the angry honking in the hellish traffic to reassure them, should any doubts have lingered, of the rightness of their decision to leave. She is not sure what they are hoping for, or what they might find too loathsome to behold.

Beirut is still alive, in one of her many transformations, still sandwiched between mountains and sea. Something else is unchanged: the ever-hovering shadow of a war they all remember, even the young who, although they didn't experience the full-scale violence of the civil war, grew up amidst assassinations and clashes. They live with the feeling that they continue to endure, that peace is a long way away. She sees the war in the young men who remind her of other youngsters whose living quarters she had briefly shared, reckless and loud, beside themselves with frustration at the few possibilities available. A matter of time, perhaps. Yet she prefers to think they have been effectively inoculated, that the madness of those times is forever behind them.

She likes the clean-cut, mild-mannered, college-educated sons and daughters of her friends, and yet they, too, can profoundly shock her. The Iraq war, of course they condone it while sipping their Châteauneuf-du-Pape and making plans to go off to Dubai to sign lucrative contracts, and the American empire, and Israel as a counterpoint to backwards, stick-in-the-mud Islam that would have them all living in the dark ages. Of course she is not pleased with the outcome of the civil war, the Christians' power greatly diminished. But her own life has barely been altered as a result. She skis and dines out and travels, although she knows she is one of the lucky few who still can.

Nothing has changed. The same men still in power, and if not they, then their sons and their grandsons. She brings this, along with her bag of goodies. And wounds unhealed. Why should her family greet her with open arms?

And yet, if they have not reckoned with the past, at least they are wary of repeating it, and this might be their only salvation.

How seduced she had been, back at the hotel, by the maid's effectiveness at straightening the mess she had managed to create in such a short time. (Carmen was her name. Eva has left her a good tip, even though Carmen had complained about the smoking in a short, curt note. Oh, Carmen! Why so picky with a name like this?) The towels would be hanging on the rack just so by the time she returned to the room, a new roll of toilet paper in the dispenser. Her propensity to create chaos could not have been accidental, and neither was Carmen's at taming it. Such was the chasm between nations. A land that cleans up after itself so efficiently deserves her profound admiration.

The seat belt light blinks and the pilot announces that they will be landing shortly and wishes them a lovely visit. Eva puts the bag of peanuts on the tray and sits up eagerly to cast her first look at Boston.

40

THE SKY HAS LIFTED and the ground sparkles with frost. A few last clouds scurry off. It is a short walk to the house now, with the sun shining and all apprehension dissolved, although it is taking them longer than it should, for they must still lumber through deep snow, and their mother walks slowly, stubbornly refusing to be carried. Behind them Loom's driveway is clear. She and George pitched in to shovel it, pausing to admire the igloo, now painted in stripes of bright colors. Finally they took leave, showering their host with their effusive thanks and an invitation to dinner.

She stops and turns to look at the igloo. She doesn't understand why he has built it, yet she is deeply touched by his act. Would she ever consider creating something of no seeming practicality, on a whim, pushed by powerful longing?

She admires Loom and feels miserable. For she will continue to dream of him from a distance. Now that she has made a fool of herself and come spectacularly out of her shell in that fleeting moment in his room and was punished severely for it (although, later, in the living room, he had been solicitous and had talked to her sweetly, she knew his consideration for what it was, pity), she will never go near him again, and will flee to her room if indeed, as he assured them before they left, he will accept their invitation to dinner, he's not sure yet about next week, but one of these days, definitely. She did not dare look in his direction at dinner last night, and played with the food on her plate, waiting miserably for it to be over and for him to assign their sleeping arrangements. For they'd had to spend the night, the wind having increased dangerously, preventing them from leaving. He'd been gracious, not once making them feel unwelcome. In the end, she'd slept fitfully on the rug by the fire next to Marie while her mother took the sofa and her brother and Salma occupied the single bed in the guest room. She heard him pacing in his room, and once he even came downstairs and went outside for a few moments. She guessed that he was worried about the mound. Judging from the racket, the wind must have been causing damage. The first thing she did this morning was look out the window. She was hugely relieved to find the mound intact. It was now a full-fledged igloo with an entrance already carved. There were broken branches lying on the ground, and a few young trees had been completely uprooted.

He was kind again this morning before they left. Shook their hands and said he might see them soon. Waved off their eager thanks once again, as if this were the least he could do.

She knows she is unattractive. She wonders what people see when they look at her. If her loneliness is written over her face, keeping strangers away lest they get trapped into giving solace.

How she wishes she could take back that moment of foolishness in Loom's room!

And yet. It was the push they might have all needed, her mother fleeing in the storm. She looks around and takes a deep breath. The day after a storm is really a glorious sight. All these years, holed up in their house as if they were still in Beirut, barricaded behind sand bags. She thanks her mother silently.

She hopes he will come to dinner. No, she will not flee to her room but will be a perfect host. Next to George and Marie, she speaks the best English. She will not get her hopes foolishly up, but will simply be happy with his presence, when and if he decides to come.

Their house is near now. Eva might be coming today, tomorrow at the latest, as soon as the flights have resumed. She draws level with her mother and hooks her arm with hers. She remembers walking with her mother in one of the old souks of Beirut before the war. She had been scolded for going off on her own into the narrow mazes of the old market, drawn by the colorful displays and the vendors shouting out their wares. When her mother found her, she gave her a spanking. After a while, her tears had dried up and she had been offered apricot ice cream for consolation. And there, in the old market where the noises and smells of the crowd both repulsed and drew her in, her hand firmly planted in her mother's and apricot ice cream sticky on her fingers, she had felt herself, despite the spanking and the desire, still, to let go of her mother's hand and wander off into the boisterous, impossible market, the luckiest girl on earth.

She was cruel to Michel. Maybe she had also been cruel to Eva. She chose dead leaves under a lemon tree on which to cut out the past, trembling at the magnitude of her breach, while Eva had chosen glamorous nightclubs and powerful men. But they had both been drunk with the thought that, briefly, they were allowed to do what they pleased while the world ended around them.

She invents their encounter: a car honks its horn, there's the sound of doors slamming. They scurry to the window. There is Eva, tipping the taxi driver, dressed in brown, and in heels too high for the weather. For a moment, she stands still and gazes at the house. The sun shines on the walkway, which George has just finished shoveling. Loom's igloo stands at the edge of their vision. Eva bends over and picks up her suitcases. She is here, Josephine tells her mother, and at once they straighten their backs and walk out to greet her.